Wedding Cake

Center Point
Large Print

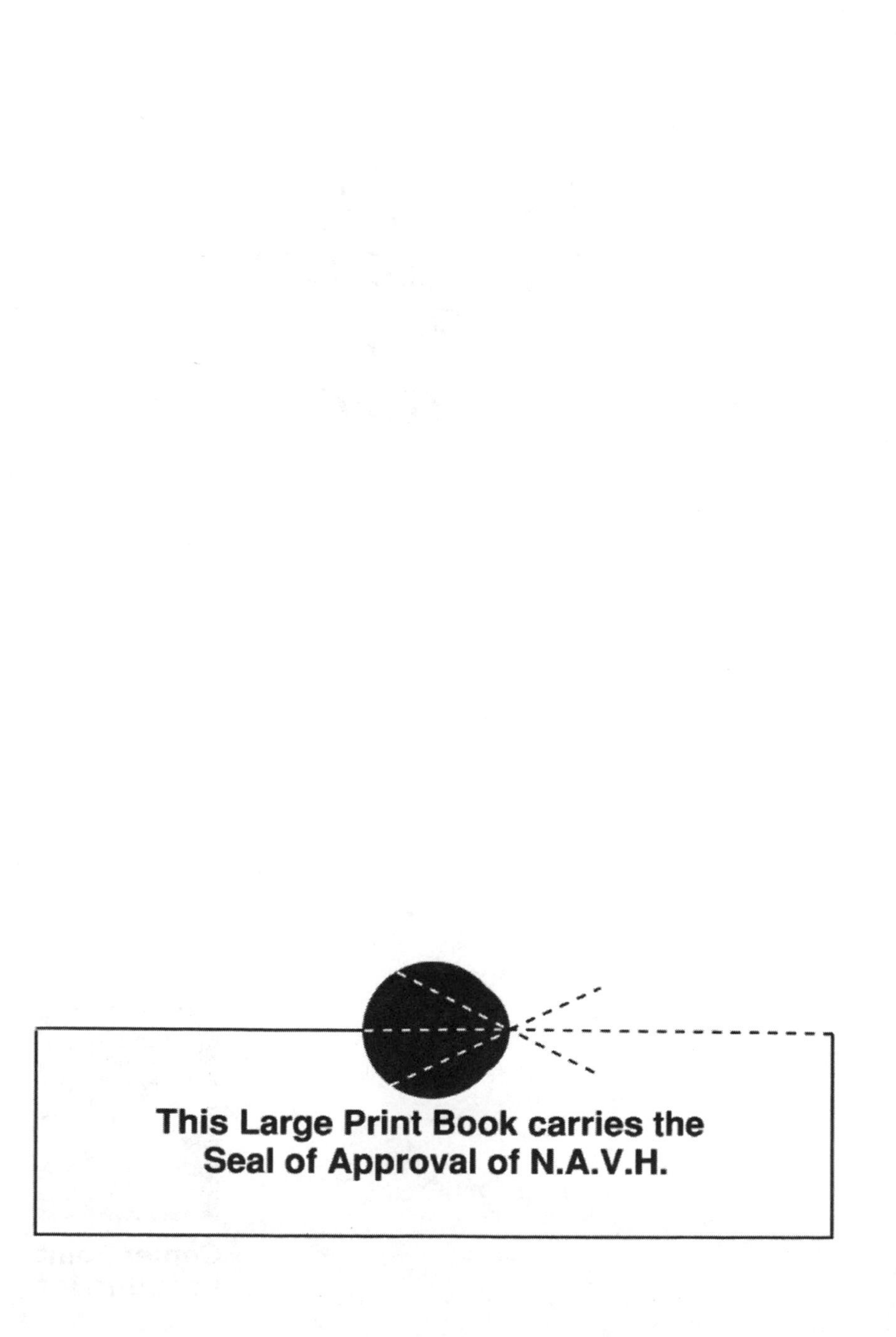
This Large Print Book carries the
Seal of Approval of N.A.V.H.

Wedding Cake

LYNNE HINTON

CENTER POINT PUBLISHING
THORNDIKE, MAINE

This Center Point Large Print edition
is published in the year 2010 by arrangement with
Avon Books, an imprint of HarperCollins Publishers.

This book is a work of fiction. The characters,
incidents, and dialogue are drawn from the author's
imagination and are not to be construed as real.
Any resemblance to actual events or persons,
living or dead, is entirely coincidental.

The text of this Large Print edition is unabridged.
In other aspects, this book may vary
from the original edition.
Printed in the United States of America
on permanent paper.
Set in 16-point Times New Roman type.

ISBN: 978-1-60285-853-4

Library of Congress Cataloging-in-Publication Data

Hinton, J. Lynne.
Wedding cake / Lynne Hinton.
p. cm.
ISBN 978-1-60285-853-4 (library binding : alk. paper)
1. Female friendship—Fiction 2. Church membership—Fiction
3. North Carolina—Fiction. 4. Large type books. I. Title.
PS3558.I457W43 2010b
813′.54—dc22

2010016144

For Isabella Valcárcel,
Gator girl, treasured friend,
law school bound.

Acknowledgments

Thank you to Wendy Lee, fabulous editor, and Sally McMillan, trusted agent and friend.

I am thankful for the gift of bcing able to share this story and to everyone willing to read it. I am truly blessed.

Recipes

Cheese Balls

1 stick butter, softened
1 cup flour
pinch salt
1 cup grated medium-sharp cheese

Mix with hands and roll into small balls. Bake 10 to 15 minutes on ungreased cookie sheet at 400 degrees.

—Beatrice Witherspoon

Chapter One

"Charlotte speaking." Charlotte Stewart was answering the phone at the women's shelter where she worked as the executive director because Maria, the office volunteer, had gone into town to buy some stamps.

"So, how did it go?"

Charlotte smiled at the voice on the other end of the telephone. "Beatrice Newgarden Witherspoon, please tell me that you have not invested any of your money in starting a matchmaking service because you are really, really unqualified to handle these things." Charlotte waited for the response. She always loved talking to her former parishioner and old friend.

"It was the hairpiece that threw you off, wasn't it? I tried to tell him that in today's time, bald is in."

Beatrice had discovered that her husband's boss, the owner of the funeral home in Hope Springs, North Carolina, had a nephew who was going to a conference in Albuquerque, New Mexico. She had met Rollin Fair a couple of times, and she knew he had gotten divorced and had been single for a few months. She just thought it was part of her Christian duty to help love along. Since Charlotte, her former pastor, was heading toward forty and was still single, and was conveniently located in Gallup, New Mexico, just a couple of hours away from the winter gathering of the National Funeral Directors Conference, it seemed inspired.

Rollin wasn't really a great catch, but Bea knew that he was gainfully employed, had his own house, and, best of all, was located back in North Carolina. Besides, Dick, her husband, had told her that Rollin was a becoming a fine funeral director and a good businessman, in line to take over the family business. He had an excellent retirement package and a wonderful time-share rental in south Florida. Beatrice considered these to be honorable attributes and began making calls to Charlotte and to Rollin as soon as she heard that the divorce was final and that he was going to the conference out west. Besides, she was not ashamed of the fact that she was acting a little selfishly since she thought that if she could find her former pastor a love interest back in North Carolina, maybe Charlotte might come back home. Charlotte had finally agreed to go out with Rollin just to get Beatrice to leave her alone. The one blind date had been a catastrophe.

"No, I'm sorry to say that the hairpiece was not the worst part of the evening."

"Oh dear." Beatrice sighed. "He talked about his ex-wife, didn't he?" Dick had also mentioned that the divorce had been a result of his wife having an affair and that Rollin was having a difficult time of it.

"For two hours straight. Beatrice, the man is a mess. Why on earth did you think we would enjoy each other's company?"

"It just seemed ordained," she answered.

"Ordained?" Charlotte asked. "Trust me, this was not ordained. Unless you think he needed a counselor, which, I would add, he certainly does."

"Well, maybe when he gets over his grief, you'll reconsider." Beatrice remained hopeful.

"I somehow think that's not happening anytime soon. In fact, if I wait around for him to get back to normal, I've got a feeling I'll be coming to him for his professional services, meaning one of us will be on our deathbed."

Beatrice laughed. "It was that bad, huh?"

"It was terrible." Charlotte paused.

"Well, I'll send you the money for the gas it took for you to drive to Albuquerque. And I'll just keep looking for you."

"No!" Charlotte quickly replied. "Please, don't set me up with anybody else."

"But dear, I feel that it's my duty as your friend to help you find true love. I've already signed you up for one of those Internet dating services for people in the South. In fact, that was another reason I was calling. I need a few details." Beatrice reached over and pulled out a file she had near the phone. She cleared her throat. "Do you have any prior convictions or have you ever had any sexually transmitted diseases?"

"Beatrice!" Charlotte yelled the name so loudly that one of the women walking by her office stopped and peeked in to make sure the executive director was okay. Charlotte smiled at the client and nodded, showing that she was just fine. "Beatrice, take my name off of that service. The last thing I need is to have some crazy man showing up at the shelter!"

"Oh, you're right. I forgot about where you are now." Beatrice blew out a breath. "Hey, how about any of those contacts? Do any of your women know anybody that could be a potential husband for you?"

Charlotte laughed. "Bea, these are survivors of domestic abuse. I don't really think I want them hooking me up, if you know what I mean."

"Right," Beatrice agreed.

"Besides," Charlotte noted, "I have met someone."

"Who? Where?" Beatrice sounded excited.

Charlotte let out a heavy sigh. She had not intended to say anything to anybody, and particularly not to Beatrice. Even though she was a couple thousand miles away, Beatrice had a way of meddling that went beyond even great distances. "He's a police officer. He's from here," she added.

"A policeman?" Beatrice asked. "You're not paying off a parking ticket with sex, are you?"

"Bea, what is wrong with you?"

"I'm just asking."

"No, Bea, I am not paying him off with sex." Charlotte shook her head.

"Okay," Beatrice responded, and then waited. "Then he's not one of those dirty cops who takes money from strip club owners to look the other way when they're running a prostitution ring, is he?"

"What? No." Charlotte already regretted telling Beatrice the news. "Are you still getting HBO and not paying for it?"

"I'm still considering my entertainment options," Beatrice replied. "And I have seen plenty of programs about bad cops."

"He's not a bad cop," Charlotte responded. "He's a good guy." She thought about him, how he had smiled at her as they stood at her doorstep the night before when they went out on their second date. She remembered how kind he had been, how sweet. She blushed recalling the innocent kiss he had planted on her cheek.

"You're thinking about him now, aren't you?" Beatrice asked, aware of the sudden pause in the conversation.

Charlotte sat up in her chair, looking like she had just gotten caught by the high school principal for making out in the hallway. "I'm sorry, did you ask a question, Bea?"

"Are you going to tell me about him?"

Charlotte thought for a minute. "There's not a lot to tell right now. We've only been out twice. His name is Donovan and he is Navajo."

"Navajo? Like an Indian, Navajo?"

"Yes, like an Indian Navajo," Charlotte answered.

"An Indian named Donovan?"

"Yes, Beatrice, an Indian named Donovan."

"Hmmmmm," Beatrice responded.

"So, what else is going on in Hope Springs?" Charlotte asked, changing the subject.

Beatrice sighed. She knew Charlotte was through talking about her new boyfriend. She was hoping for more information, but she would let Charlotte have her way now and would ask more questions later. She decided to go along with the new subject. "Louise heard from George."

"Who's George?" Charlotte asked, glad to have moved on.

"You know, the husband of Roxie, that woman she loved from her teenage years, the one she had move in with her when she got Alzheimer's."

Charlotte knew the name Roxie very well. She remembered how Louise Fisher, another woman from Hope Springs, had confessed her love for her oldest friend and how she wanted nothing more than to care for her, love her, be with her while she was dying. Roxie's family allowed Louise to take her into her home because none of them, especially her husband, who was having an affair at the time, wanted the responsibility of caring for the dying woman.

"Why on earth did he contact Louise?" Charlotte asked. She recalled that George had never been very fond of Roxie's best friend. Even Louise had said that he had always been suspicious of the friendship between his wife and the single woman from North Carolina. They had been civil with each other only because of Roxie, the woman they both loved. She had asked them to try and get along, so they had. When Roxie developed dementia, Louise and George had fought long and hard about her care.

"I'm not sure," Beatrice answered. "Lou only said that he was planning a trip south and that he wanted to stop by and see her."

Charlotte knew that Roxie's family was from the Baltimore area. She remembered being with Louise after the funeral and how the friends from Hope Springs, calling themselves the cookbook committee because of their efforts to produce a church cookbook, drove together to Baltimore at Christmas to be with Louise at the time of Roxie's death.

"Well, that's weird," Charlotte noted. "How long has it been since that funeral?"

"It seems forever," Beatrice replied. "It seems a lot longer than Margaret's."

There was a pause in the conversation as both women thought of their very dear friend Margaret

Peele. It had been only a few months since Margaret's death, and all the women on the cookbook committee, all the friends, still grieved deeply over their common loss.

"You remember how Margaret got us to Baltimore?" Beatrice made a sort of clucking noise. "She was worried to death about Louise, called us to come up there and help."

"As I recall, neither you nor Jessie needed a lot of convincing," Charlotte said. "The two of you were packed and in that car before I even knew what was going on."

"You went with us too," Beatrice said. There was a softness in her voice. "I don't remember much hesitation from you either."

Charlotte smiled. She had always loved that cookbook committee, loved every one of its members: Jessie Jenkins, with her bold and brassy friendship; Louise, and her wonderful and attentive ways of caring; even Beatrice, the biggest busybody she knew . . . still, Beatrice had the biggest heart of all of them. Those women had taught Charlotte a lot about being the woman she wanted to be. But Margaret, Margaret had always been the special one of the group to Charlotte. Charlotte's mother was still alive but the minister had never felt the same closeness with her own kin that she felt for her parishioner Margaret. The tears began to gather in her eyes. She still had a hard time talking about the woman who had taught her wisdom and strength and the true meaning of courage.

"We are quite the committee," Charlotte said, reaching for a tissue.

"Yes, we are," Beatrice agreed, sharing a few tears of her own. "Which is why we still have a commitment to each other."

"Anything any of us needs," Charlotte responded.

"Which is why I'm working so hard to get you married," Beatrice added.

Charlotte laughed. "Beatrice Witherspoon, what am I ever to do with you?"

"Well, I'm going to hang up for now because I know you're busy, but the next time we talk, I expect a full report on your Officer Love."

"Donovan," Charlotte said. "Donovan Sanchez."

Beatrice waited. "Officer Donovan Sanchez," she repeated. "Is that Spanish? What, is he biracial? Does he speak English?"

"Yes, Bea, he speaks English."

Beatrice made a sort of humming noise. She wasn't sure how she felt about this news. Even though she had talked to all their friends and knew that Charlotte was very happy in New Mexico, she had never given up hope that the young woman would get her fill of the Southwest and move back to North Carolina. The news that Charlotte had found love out where she was living hurt those odds.

"Did I mention that Rollin has a time-share in Miami? He gets two weeks a year at a condo right on the beach. I could call him up for you, help him find some counseling. Maybe they can do some of that electric shock therapy, like I saw on a documentary last week about people addicted to that new drug mets or something, and then you can go out with him again when he gets fixed up?"

"The drug is called meth and I don't think so. But you're kind to ask. However, I don't really think me and Mr. Fair Jr. have much of a future together."

"All right, I'll not speak of him again."

"Thank you, Beatrice."

"You are welcome, Pastor Charlotte. But the next time we talk, I do expect more information about your Officer Sanchez."

"Fair enough."

"Love you, Charlotte."

"Love you too, Bea."

And the two women hung up their phones.

Cheese Cocktail Crackers

1 cup (½ pound) margarine, melted
2 cups sifted flour
⅓ cup sugar
1 teaspoon salt
1 cup grated cheddar cheese
1 cup chopped pecans

Blend margarine, flour, sugar, and salt until fine particles are created. Add cheese and blend. Mix in chopped pecans. Shape dough into a long roll 1½ inches in diameter. Wrap roll in waxed paper. Chill. Cut into ⅛-inch slices. Bake at 350 degrees for 10 to 15 minutes. Makes 6 dozen.

—Jessie Jenkins

Chapter Two

"An Indian police officer?" Jessie was cleaning up the dishes from breakfast. It was late morning, but she had gone walking right after finishing the meal. She had just gotten around to straightening up when Beatrice stopped by.

"Navajo," Beatrice replied. She had decided to visit her friend after she had spoken to Charlotte. "Do you think I should get a rundown, do a 411 on him?"

Jessie turned to Beatrice. "Are you still stealing those cable programs?"

Beatrice rolled her eyes and sat down at the table. "I am not stealing programs. I just want to try them out before we pay for them."

Jessie shot her friend a look of suspicion. "How much did you pay the television repairman to let you try it out?"

"Fifty bucks and it was his idea. I have always intended to pay for it once I decide whether or not I like the shows he got me."

"Uh-huh." Jessie went back to drying her dishes at the sink.

"Besides, the young man needed a little extra cash. I was just trying to help him out a bit. You know Discount Danny doesn't pay his workers enough money. That's why they keep leaving him and going to work for Sears."

"Danny pays his employees a fair price. He was the only white businessman to hire an African-American salesman. It was James Jr.'s first job and he worked for him a number of years. He's a good man and an ethical businessman. He treated me and my family with the same respect he treated the white folks in this town. And I don't think he would be too happy if he knew his crew was providing his customers with illegal services."

"Getting the Weather Channel is illegal?" Beatrice asked, trying to sound innocent.

"It is if you aren't a paying customer." Jessie put the plates in the cabinet and dried off two coffee cups. She placed one in front of Beatrice. "How does that work anyway? How did he hook you up without having you register?"

"I don't ask those kinds of questions," Bea answered, taking the cup and sounding smug. She reached over and poured the coffee for herself from the pot that was placed in the center of the table. She took a spoonful of sugar and stirred it in. "He had some computer thingie that he slipped in the back of the television. I wasn't watching so that I won't need to lie if the cable people question me. But never you mind. I'm going to figure out which channels I want and I will have Lester come back and unhook me and then I'll call the cable company and upgrade my order."

"Uh-huh," Jessie responded. She sat down across

from her friend and poured a cup of coffee for herself. "Well, enough about your illegal activities. I don't want to become an accessory to your bad behavior. Tell me more about Charlotte and her new love."

"I don't know a lot," Beatrice replied. "Yet," she added. "But I intend to find out more as soon as I can." She thought about her earlier conversation. "I must say, though, she sounded smitten."

"Smitten?" Jessie repeated. "I can't say as I have ever heard Charlotte sound smitten." She shook her head. "A Navajo police officer." She smiled. "And she sounds smitten."

"Yes, and he has a Spanish last name," Beatrice noted as she drank a sip of coffee and then placed her cup in front of her.

"How did they meet?" Jessie asked, leaning back in her chair.

"Don't know," Beatrice answered.

"How many times have they gone out?" Jessie asked.

"Two, I think," Beatrice said.

Jessie nodded her head, taking in the information. "Well, good for her," she responded.

"Well, let's hope it's good for her," Beatrice said, sounding concerned.

"Beatrice, finding a boyfriend for Charlotte has been all you have talked about for months. I thought you would be happy for her."

"I'm not saying I'm not happy." She leaned up

and rested her chin on her fists. "I'm just saying I think she should go a little more slowly."

"What?" Jessie asked, sounding very surprised. "You think somebody should go slowly? When have you ever gone slowly about anything? After all, you're the one who got us all to shave our heads for Margaret before we found out that she wasn't going to have chemotherapy. You're the one who started that cookbook and that Christmas Cake Recipe Contest before you ever thought about how much work those projects would be. You're the one who got a funeral van to drive Margaret back to Texas last year. You are not somebody with qualifications to hand out advice about slowing down!"

Beatrice blew out a long breath. "I did not come over here for a lecture," she said. "I just came to let you know what I had heard. I thought you would be as concerned as I am."

Jessie smiled. "Oh Beatrice, Charlotte has a boyfriend. Be glad for her. She would never pick a bad guy. I'm sure we will like him as much as she does when we get the chance to meet him." She took a sip of her coffee. "This has gotten cold. You want me to brew another pot?"

Beatrice was looking down. She shook her head.

"What?" Jessie asked. She could see her friend was upset about something.

"She's never coming back, is she?" Beatrice looked up at Jessie.

Jessie reached over and took her by the hands. "That's what this is about, isn't it?" She smiled at Beatrice. "You wanted to find Charlotte a boyfriend back here so that she would move home."

"Well, I don't see what's so wrong with that," Beatrice responded. "Robin still doesn't ever come home to visit. Teddy has gotten some teaching fellowship in Japan, and Jenny and the twins are so busy in their own lives," she said, speaking about her children and grandchildren. "Louise is all wrapped up in her gardening classes and now talking about Roxie all over again. You and James stay completely involved in the lives of your children and grandchildren. Dick works all the time. Margaret is—" She stopped and took a breath. She still missed her friend so much. "I just thought it would be nice to have Charlotte back," she confessed. "Even if she doesn't want to be our preacher again, she could come back and be our friend."

Jessie nodded. "It would be nice." She also thought about Margaret and how empty life seemed without her. She understood Beatrice's reasons for wanting their young friend back in their shrinking circle. "But Charlotte has made her own life in New Mexico. And we get to see her once in a while. I miss her too. But she's happy out there, and she's doing very good work at that shelter."

Beatrice pulled her hands away and reached over and got a napkin. She dabbed at her eyes. "Well, that's true. She does seem happy helping out those women." She paused. "But we got women who get beat up here too," she noted.

"That's true," Jessie responded. "Sad, but true. However, I don't think Charlotte moved to New Mexico just to find abused women." She sat back in her chair.

"Why do you think she went out there?" Beatrice asked. She folded her arms across her waist. "Do you think she was unhappy here?"

Jessie shrugged. "I don't know exactly. I do know that there was a time when I wanted to move and live somewhere else."

"But you didn't, and now you're glad you stayed, right?" Beatrice remembered hearing about Jessie's wanderlust and how she had wanted to live in another place when she was younger.

"I am glad I'm here now, but I still think I would have enjoyed living in another place for a while. But once the children were born and then when James left, I just couldn't imagine going anywhere else." Jessie glanced out the window, remembering how it was for her when her husband walked out on her. He was gone for a lot of years before he came back.

"How long have you guys been married?" Beatrice asked.

Jessie thought about the question and counted up the years. "Well, if you add all of the years together, since we never really got divorced, it would be fifty years. But if you take away the years that he was gone it would be less."

"Which one do you count?" Beatrice asked.

"I think the first one, the long one, because even though we weren't together for all those years, I still felt married to him, still connected to him. He has always been my husband even when he wasn't here."

Beatrice perked up. "You should have a vow renewal service," she announced.

"A what?" Jessie asked.

"A second wedding," Bea answered. "A ceremony where you and James renew your vows. I mean, he came back and you took him in but you didn't have an event of any kind to celebrate." She clapped her hands together. "We can do it at the church. I'm sure Reverend Joles will be happy to do it. No!" She stopped and looked directly at Jessie. "We can ask Charlotte to come back and officiate! That way we can look into her eyes when she talks about her officer and we'll know for sure if he's right for her." She stopped and gasped. "We could even make her bring him with her! We get to plan a party *and* find out the truth about Charlotte."

"Wait, wait, Bea." Jessie put up her hand. "Let's just take a minute to think about this. A second wedding? Charlotte coming back to officiate?" She shook her head. "I'm not sure this is something James and I would want."

"What wouldn't I want?" James had come into the house and was standing at the back door.

Both women turned to look in his direction.

"Hey babe," Jessie called out.

"Hey babe," Beatrice repeated.

"Hello, my lovely women," James responded. "And what are the two of you cooking up?" He reached down and gave Jessie a kiss on the forehead, then turned around and walked over to the cabinets to get a coffee cup. He headed back over to the table and squeezed Beatrice on the shoulders.

"We are going to plan a second wedding for you and Jessie and we're going to invite Charlotte to come back and officiate!" Beatrice was all aglow with her new idea. "That will give us the chance to meet Charlotte's new beau and spend time with her, maybe make her stay here, and celebrate something wonderful: your love!"

James turned to his wife and winked. Then he poured himself a cup of coffee and leaned against the kitchen counter. He took a sip while both women waited for his response. Beatrice was especially eager to hear his reaction.

"I think it's a great idea," he remarked with a grin.

"Really?" Jessie asked, surprised.

"Really," he replied. "After fifty years I would like nothing more than to tell the world that I am marrying you all over again."

Jessie blushed. A big smile swept across her face.

Beatrice rubbed her hands together. "Okay, we'll need to get invitations and pick a date. We need to reserve the church and the fellowship hall."

"I think I'd rather do it here," Jessie said. She was starting to enjoy the idea.

Beatrice glanced around. "Inside or out?" she asked.

James and Jessie looked at each other and at the same time answered, "Out."

Beatrice grinned. "An outdoor wedding." She thought about the logistics of planning the event. "Summer then?" she asked.

"Late spring," Jessie replied.

"May," James added. "Our anniversary is in May." He took another sip of coffee and winked again at his wife.

"May it is," Beatrice exclaimed. "Oh my, there's so much to do and not a lot of time to do it in. We'll need to think about flowers and music and a photographer and a honeymoon." She pushed her chair away from the table. "And, oh my, I have another fabulous idea!"

"What?" Jessie asked.

"How about putting together a wedding

cookbook?" she asked, her face flushed with excitement.

And both Jessie and James turned to their friend in exasperation and yelled at the same time, *"No cookbook!"*

Chili Dip

1 15-ounce can chili without beans
1 cup shredded cheddar cheese
hot sauce to taste
½ teaspoon cayenne pepper

Combine all ingredients. Heat until cheese melts. Serve hot with tortilla chips. Makes 2 cups.

—Maria Roybal

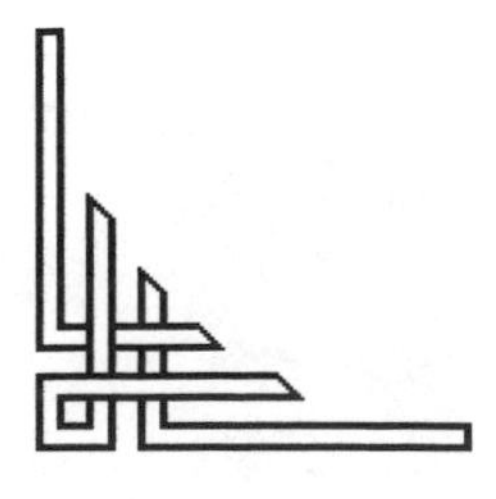

Chapter Three

Charlotte was staring out the window and still thinking about Beatrice and their conversation, how she had spilled the beans and told her about Donovan, whom she had only gone out with a couple of times. She was having her regrets when Maria walked into the office. When Charlotte turned around, the shelter volunteer was standing right in front of the desk, wearing a strange look on her face.

"Hello Maria, how was it?" Charlotte asked. She could tell that Maria definitely had something to tell her.

Maria remained standing very close to Charlotte. She placed the stamps on the corner of the desk and then looked back up. "I went to the post office," she responded.

Charlotte smiled. She loved how dramatic the volunteer could be at times. "Yes, I remember where you were going. And you got stamps too, which is fabulous, Maria. Is that the reason for that goofy look on your face? Are they special stamps?" She glanced over to the small roll that had been placed by the phone. They seemed to be the same U.S. flag variety that she was used to having.

"Did we get a discount?" Charlotte knew how

Maria loved to use coupons and ask vendors for discounts.

"I do not wear this look about my face because of stamps." Maria waited, allowing for the dramatic pause.

"Okay." Charlotte played along.

She and Maria had been friends for almost three years. Maria was one of the first people she had met when she moved to Gallup, and Maria's family had sort of adopted Charlotte since her arrival. Charlotte ate at least one meal a week with the Roybal family. She babysat Maria's grandchildren from time to time and even attended Mass with them once or twice a month. Maria and her husband, Gilbert, were helping Charlotte with her language skills in Spanish.

"Well, are you going to tell me or do you want me to keep guessing?" Charlotte asked. "I've got work to do, Maria," she added.

"I ran into Isabella Gomez while I was standing in line to buy the stamps."

Charlotte thought that the name sounded familiar but she didn't think she knew who Maria was talking about. She shrugged.

Maria sighed as if she thought Charlotte ought to know who Isabella was. "Isabella Gomez is married to Daniel Gomez, and his sister married Jimmie Lujan from Farmington," Maria explained. "They sit in the fourth row at Mass every Sunday."

"Isabella and Daniel, or Jimmie Lujan?"

Maria let out another sigh. "Isabella and Daniel." She thought for a moment. "She stacks her hair really high and adds a bun extension to the top of her head."

"A bun or a French twist?" Charlotte asked, thinking about the women's hairstyles she had seen in the Catholic church.

"Bun," Maria answered, growing impatient.

"Okay," Charlotte said, nodding her head. "And this is important because?"

"This is important because Daniel's sister's husband, Jimmie Lujan, has a cousin who is married to Carla Fairhope."

There was another pause. Charlotte shook her head, hoping Maria would soon get to her point.

"Yes, and?" Charlotte asked.

"And Carla Fairhope is really Carla Sanchez Fairhope."

Charlotte still was not following Maria's line of conversation. She waited.

"Carla *Sanchez* Fairhope," Maria repeated, very carefully sounding out the name.

"Carla Sanchez Fairhope," Charlotte said. And then the name finally rang a bell. "Are you trying to tell me that she is somehow related to Donovan?"

Charlotte had told her friend about meeting the Gallup policeman and about their first date, and Maria had promised, without any urging or request from Charlotte, to find out everything she could about the New Mexico native.

"Oh, she's more than just related." She paused, wanting even more of a dramatic effect to what she was about to say.

Charlotte leaned in, waiting. "What, Maria?" she finally asked.

Maria glanced around to see if anyone was outside in the hall.

Charlotte followed her eyes. She whispered, "It's just us. The women have all gone to job training at the community college, and the kids are in school."

Maria nodded again, looking as if she wanted to be very careful with her news.

Charlotte shrugged, still waiting.

"She was his first wife." Maria punctuated the end of the sentence with a loud bang on the desk, pounding her fist. And then she stood up straight and waited for Charlotte's response.

Charlotte was surprised to hear this news, but it didn't shock her as much as it apparently shocked Maria. She and Donovan had not spoken to each other about past relationships, so it wasn't as if he had lied to her or kept anything from her. She knew that if they continued to see each other, this subject would certainly come up, but at this point, she hadn't asked him a lot of personal questions.

"So, he's divorced?" Charlotte asked, not showing nearly the amount of emotion that Maria was expecting.

"You are not upset?"

"He's in his forties, Maria. It shouldn't surprise you that a man his age has been married before." She reached over to a folder and opened it. There were some forms she needed to fill out and get in the afternoon mail; that was part of the reason she had sent Maria to get stamps. As always in non-profit work, a deadline was looming.

"You didn't find out from him if he had ever been married?" Maria asked. She pulled up a chair and sat across from Charlotte, surprised to see that her friend wasn't stunned about this important bit of news.

"No, Maria, I didn't ask him if he had ever been married. We've only been out twice." Charlotte looked back down at the form. It was from the state government, requesting the number of children served by St. Mary's House in the last quarter and their ages, as well as other information about them. The women's shelter received a certain amount of money based on the clientele they served. These forms were always important to complete because the funds were a necessary part of their income.

Maria studied the young woman. She made a kind of humming noise.

Charlotte glanced up. "What?"

"There are things you should always ask right off the bat when you go out with a man."

"Things?" Charlotte repeated.

"Things," Maria answered, nodding.

"Besides having been married before, what other things?" Charlotte asked. This interested her.

"Any known children, medical and family history, religious preferences, mental illnesses . . ." She stopped to consider other issues. "And any bad debts," she added.

"Wow," Charlotte responded. "That's a lot of information. Maybe I need to ask the state to make forms for my dates." She held up the paper she was working on and shook her head; the entire dialogue she was having was starting to sound and feel very familiar. "You are as bad as Beatrice Witherspoon," she commented, remembering the conversation she had just had with her former church member. "I'm not asking all of those questions on the first date. And besides, it doesn't matter to me if he's been married before," she added.

Maria blew out a breath. "Your friend is right to worry about you. *Los hombres que te ocultan una cosa, te ocultaran muchas más.*"

"Maria, you know how bad my Spanish is. I heard 'men' and 'keep things.' What are you saying?"

"All I'm saying is that you need to beware of Mr. Donovan Sanchez."

Charlotte laughed. "Because he didn't tell me he has been married?"

"Is he hiding anything else?" Maria asked, looking very suspicious.

"You mean like mental illness and bad debt?"

"You go ahead and make fun. These are things every woman should know about a man she sees socially."

"Are you watching a lot of television these days?" Charlotte asked, thinking of Beatrice and all her crime movie talk.

"I watch *La Fea Más Bella* but I don't see what that has to do with this conversation."

"Well, maybe you watch too much *La Fea Más Bella*."

"I still say if you have been married before, that information should come up during a date."

"Maria, the first time we went out was just for coffee after I got a flat tire and he helped me change it. We were together for just one hour. We talked about our jobs, cars, the weather, football, and whether we prefer green or red chile. Then the next time, our first real date, we went to see a movie together, so we didn't chat at all while we were in the theater, and after that we had ice cream and talked about what makes us laugh. We didn't get into past relationships!"

"And?" Maria asked.

"And what?" Charlotte replied.

"And which does he prefer?" Maria still had her arms folded across her chest. She was not letting go of her suspicions.

Charlotte shook her head, not understanding the question.

"Green or red?" Maria asked, smiling.

Charlotte laughed. "Whichever is hottest," she replied.

Maria nodded in approval. "Okay, so he got that one right," she said. "Any real New Mexican knows that even though usually the red chile is hotter, you always ask the restaurant server because it isn't a hard and fast rule. The temperature of the peppers has to do with the batch from which they come, not so much with the color."

She straightened the folds in her dress, smoothing the wrinkles down with the palms of her hands. "I just think you need to check up on these men before you spend too much time together."

"And why would I need to do that when I have such attentive women in my life who know so much about policemen and dating and divorces and can find out so much more information than I ever could?" Charlotte smiled at her friend.

"You make fun if you want to, but you just look around and remember where you are." Maria clasped her hands in her lap. "I bet these girls would tell you that they wished they had asked more questions before they got involved with the men that put them here."

The older woman seemed so concerned, so worried, Charlotte knew better than to make fun anymore of Maria and her worries. Maria had become a volunteer at the women's shelter after her daughter was murdered by Maria's son-in-law. It had been a terrible time for Maria and her family, and they still grieved her death. Maria's concern for Charlotte and her other friends was real. She never wanted anyone to have to go through what her daughter and her grandchildren had been through. Domestic abuse was personal for Maria, and Charlotte understood this.

"I will talk to him about his former marriage the next time we go out," Charlotte promised, wondering if Officer Sanchez would call for another date, wondering if she would ever hear from him again.

Maria raised her eyebrows at her friend. "You want me to call Carla and ask for her side of the story?"

"No!" Charlotte answered quickly. "I don't want you to ask anybody about anything." She looked closely at her friend. "Maria?" She waited. "You hear me? No meddling."

Maria lifted her chin as if the mandate was offensive to her. "Okay, I promise. As long as you talk to him, I'll not meddle."

Charlotte stared, making sure her friend was telling her the truth. "Have you got your fingers crossed?"

Maria sighed and held out her hands in front of her, spreading her fingers. They had been crossed in her lap, and she rolled her eyes. Charlotte knew how Maria tried never to lie, but she often crossed her fingers as if that somehow made lying okay.

"I promise I will not call Carla Fairhope to ask her about her ex-husband." And she smiled. She knew that with that promise she could ask her friend Isabella anything she wanted.

Charlotte smiled in return. She wasn't duped. She knew all too well that Maria would find a way to learn everything there was to know about Donovan and his first marriage. She wouldn't have to ask him a thing. Maria would let her know the full story by her next date, if there was one.

"Would you please now go and get the latest census information from the file in the other office? If we want to get paid, I need to make sure the state gets this form back by the end of the week."

"I will be happy to do just that." Maria got up from her chair and headed out of the office. She turned back to Charlotte. "I just worry about you, Charlotte Stewart. You don't know the ways of men. I just want you to be safe."

"I know, Maria. And I love you for that. I will be careful. I promise." She winked. "My friends in North Carolina would be very glad to know I have such a devoted angel watching over me."

"Oh, they already know that," Maria said.

Charlotte seemed confused. "How would they know?" she asked.

Maria shrugged, looking innocent.

"Maria, how would they know that you watch over me?"

Maria smiled. "Why do you think Beatrice really phoned you this morning?" Maria asked.

Charlotte considered the question. "To ask about that funeral director she set me up with." She thought again. "Wait a minute. How did you know Beatrice phoned me this morning?"

"*Querida*, your friends in North Carolina have to have somebody out here that they can call and find out what's really going on with you." And with that Maria blew her friend a kiss and headed back to the other office.

"Maria," Charlotte called out.

There was no answer.

"Maria, how long have you been talking to Beatrice?" she asked, but it was too late. "Maria, don't you say anything about Donovan to anybody!" She yelled out her plea, but Maria was already well down the hall and out of range of hearing any more questions or instructions from Charlotte.

The young woman slumped in her chair, wondering about her recent phone call with Beatrice and what her friend in North Carolina already knew.

Bacon-wrapped Fried Oysters

2 eggs, beaten
¼ cup milk
2 dozen select oysters, drained
1 cup cracker meal
12 slices bacon, cut in half
olive oil

Combine eggs and milk. Dip oysters in egg mixture, then in cracker meal. Repeat process. Wrap each oyster with bacon and secure with a toothpick. Fry in shallow oil until golden. Drain on paper towel.

—Louise Fisher

Chapter Four

Louise was watching from the kitchen table when she saw the car turn into the driveway. She had been waiting and watching for more than two hours. She knew what time George had arrived at the Virginia/North Carolina border because he had called her from the rest stop at the state line. She knew from there it was at least another two hours before he would make it to Hope Springs.

Louise thought about what was happening. She'd had three phone conversations with George and she still had not figured out why he was coming to see her. The last time they had been together was at the funeral of Roxie, his wife, her best friend, and that had been almost ten years earlier. And it hadn't been such a sweet reunion even then.

Not that George and Louise were ever close. He knew Louise loved Roxie more than just as a friend and he had tried to tell his wife that Louise was dangerous with her loyalty and her love. In fact, in the beginning of his courtship with Roxie, he tried to break up the friendship, immediately casting a suspicious eye on Louise Fisher, but it never worked. Roxie and Louise had been best friends long before George entered the scene.

Roxie loved the man who would become her husband, but she told him flat-out to stay away from her friendship with Louise and that he had better learn to like her.

"Louise Fisher," she had told George on their third or fourth date, "is my family. And if you marry me, she will be your family too. So get used to it or say good-bye now."

And he had figured out a way to get used to it. He finally and ultimately accepted their friendship. He got used to it just as Louise had to get used to him and accept the fact that Roxie and George got married, moved away, and had a family, while she stayed at the cotton mill in North Carolina, alone and abandoned.

When Roxie was diagnosed with Alzheimer's, Louise had been there for her and for her family. And when George called to say that he could not care for her any longer and that he was having an affair, Louise swooped in and brought Roxie back to her home in Hope Springs. She had cared for Roxie until she died. And it was still the best thing she had ever done in her life, the best days of her life, even though they were hard and messy, and even though Roxie had only brief moments of clarity, short spans when she knew Louise and understood what was going on. Still, it had not been a burden for Louise. Taking care of Roxie, having her in her home, loving her, being with her, was still the brightest spot in life she had ever had.

She went to Maryland for the funeral, stayed with George in his home. She had helped the children go through some of Roxie's things, ate meals with them, was civil to them, loving to them, but she had not visited with or talked to George again, and her communications with Ruby and Laura, Roxie's daughters, included only cards at Christmas and an occasional birthday greeting. Once Roxie died, there had been no reason to stay in touch with her "adopted family."

She hadn't wanted the relationships to end like that but she had not been able to figure out how to do things differently. George was having his affair with some woman with whom he worked. The girls, though grown and on their own, were angry with him for leaving their mother and angry at their mother for leaving them. Louise had never known how to talk to them after Roxie died since she was still so bereaved herself, and she grieved not only the loss of her best friend, but also the loss of those girls. But it was as it was, and like everything else hard about her relationship with Roxie, she had accepted it.

And now, here was George, wanting to see her, driving all the way down to North Carolina to talk to her about something. Louise couldn't imagine what he wanted. She glanced out the window again and got up from the table and poured herself a glass of water. She considered calling Jessie or Beatrice for moral support, even considered asking them to be there with her when George arrived, but she thought better of it. She was a grown woman, she told herself, and she could manage a conversation without assistance. Besides, she knew that Jessie wouldn't say much, would stay in the background, understanding that this was Louise's situation to handle, and Beatrice wouldn't let her or George get a word in edgewise.

She stood at the window, watching the empty street, thinking about her friends and feeling grateful for them. And then she turned back and walked to the table again. Louise found herself once again missing Margaret.

If Roxie had introduced Louise to the sea that was love, Margaret had been her anchor. Friends for years, they had become like sisters, Margaret keeping Louise calm, centered. Margaret was a presence of peace and wholeness and guidance in Louise's life, and since she died, there was a large, gaping hole in Louise's heart. She thought she would never bear the loss of Roxie, but she had, and it was mostly because of Margaret. Beatrice and Jessie had helped a lot. Charlotte had been there for her too. But Margaret, Louise remembered, Margaret had held her together. Margaret had soothed her, calmed her, loved her. And since she died, Louise felt pieces of herself falling away that no one else seemed to be able to catch and hold for her the way Margaret had always seemed to be able to hold things.

She reached up and wiped away the tears. "Damn those women," she said only to herself and the spaces in her heart. "It's always the good ones who go first." She shook away the grief and saw the car pulling in the driveway. She took in a breath and walked to the front door.

George Cannon stepped out of his car and stretched. He tucked his shirt in his pants and smoothed down the sides of his curly gray hair. He looked behind him, at the street, and then up to the front porch and saw Louise standing at the top of the steps. They just stood looking at each other for a few seconds until he finally shut the car door and headed in her direction.

"Nice day for a drive," he said, taking hold of the railing and pulling himself up the steps.

"No weather up north?" Louise asked, trying to sound friendly, noticing how much Roxie's husband had aged over the years. She could see the trouble he was having getting up the steps and she wondered if something was wrong with him and that was why he had come, maybe to make some final peace with his dead wife and his dead wife's best friend.

George shook his head. When he reached the top of the landing he held out his hand. "Hello, Louise," he said, trying to catch his breath.

"George." Louise nodded and took his hand. It was an awkward moment for them both. "Come in," she said, pulling her hand away and opening the door.

George walked in behind her.

"You need to freshen up?" she asked.

He nodded, and she pointed him to the bathroom down the hall. She went into the kitchen and got out the pitcher of tea, filled two glasses with ice, poured the tea, and set the glasses on the table. She kept rearranging the pitcher and the glasses while she waited for him. Finally, George came into the kitchen and smiled.

"Iced tea," he noted. "I know I've landed south," he added.

Louise nodded and they both sat down.

"How's the girls?" Louise asked.

"Everybody's fine." He paused. "As far as I know," he added, taking a swallow of tea. "Good," he said, referring to the tea.

There was an awkward silence. Louise was at a loss in knowing how to make small talk with her best friend's widower.

"You run into much traffic?" Louise asked.

"Just around Richmond," George replied.

Another pause.

"You been doing okay?" he asked, settling into his chair.

"A few old people's ailments, cataracts, arthritis, you know, the usual, but I'm doing fine," she responded.

George smiled nervously. "I was sorry to hear about your friend," he commented.

"How did you hear about Margaret?" she asked,

not knowing how he had received news of her life and the lives of those she loved.

"I get your local paper," he replied.

Louise was surprised. "Why would you do that?" she asked. "It's a good paper, but it can't give you any better news than what you get up in Baltimore."

"I started taking it when Roxie moved here," he said. "You know, just to feel connected, I guess. I never canceled the subscription."

Louise nodded. She had never known that he had any interest in what had been going on in the town where his wife had died.

There was a pause.

"What are you doing here, George?" she finally asked, curiosity getting the best of her.

George shook his head. "That's what I always liked about you, Louise. Straight and to the point."

Louise grinned. "Well, to the point, at least."

George looked confused at first and then figured out her bit of "gay humor." He nodded.

"I'm in trouble," he confessed.

"Oh?" she asked. "And what brand of trouble do you seem to be in? Your girlfriend take you to the cleaner's?"

George looked away. "I deserve that," he said.

Louise nodded.

"We broke up a long time ago," he said. "We broke up not long after Roxie died," he added.

Louise was surprised to hear that bit of news since George had never mentioned it before. She always assumed he was glad to get rid of his first wife so that he could carry on with his lover. She just assumed that he had gotten married to the woman she had never met, the woman he had taken up with when Roxie got sick. "How come you never told me?" she asked.

He shrugged. "Didn't really think you were interested in my love life," he replied.

"Well, that's true," she noted. She took a sip of her tea. "I'm still mad at you for the affair."

George looked down. "I know you are," he responded. "I was wrong to do that to Roxie, but I was stupid and"—he shrugged—"I have to live with that. I just think I couldn't bear losing Roxie, watching her leave me a little every day."

"So you left her first?" Louise asked.

George nodded. "You took much better care of her than I would have," he confessed. "And I really think she wanted to be with you in her last days, not me."

Louise looked closely at George. In spite of how it happened, she was glad that she had been the one to care for Roxie. She suddenly realized that in some small way, she had been glad for George's affair since it did give her those final months with his wife. The realization surprised her. She decided to change the subject.

"So, if that's not your trouble, then what is?" she

asked, recalling his reason for his visit. She took another swallow of her tea.

"I'm sick," he responded. "And when I die, my money, Roxie's money, will go to the girls."

Louise nodded. "I think that's the appropriate line of things," she said. "What's wrong with you?"

"Lung cancer," he answered. "I have about a year maybe," he added. "I've been through the surgery and chemo. I even had a bout of radiation. But it's come back and it's terminal this time." He stopped for a second. This certainly explained his shortness of breath that Louise had noticed when he arrived.

Louise waited. "I'm sorry about your diagnosis," she responded, and she actually meant it.

"Thanks," he replied. "There's more. I don't want to leave all my money to the girls. The two of them getting everything would be the appropriate line of things except Ruby married a complete loser."

Louise listened. She had known Ruby's husband and was not particularly thrilled with him, but she certainly wouldn't have called him a loser exactly. She had always thought Ruby and her husband made a nice couple.

"He's got real problems. He gambles and he refuses to get help. Ruby is in a major state of denial about it. I don't want him to get any of our money. Ted has already been nosing around about how much he would inherit, and Ruby doesn't seem to care that he'll take it all and blow it on booze and horses. Frankly, I think she may be drinking herself. And Laura's got so much money she doesn't need any of it. And I just don't want to see it go to waste." He took a breath and looked intently at Louise. "I don't want them to squander what Roxie and I worked so hard to save."

Louise shrugged. "So change your will, give the money to a charity. Tell your daughters it's for their children. There are lots of options of how to fix this to be the way you want it."

George nodded. "I've thought of all of that. But there always seems to be some way that Ted can figure out how to get the money or at least get into the house and steal everything. And if I'm sick, who's to say he won't squander it all before I die? I mean, even if I took them out of the will, one of the girls will have to have my health care power of attorney, and they could wipe me out while I'm still alive."

"Okay, George, so you've got all of this trouble with your money and your girls. I still don't understand why you're here to see me." Louise wanted answers.

"I came to see if you would marry me," he said.

Louise couldn't believe what she had just heard and she began to choke. She coughed and sputtered, knocking over her glass as she reached for a napkin. George jumped up from his seat and stood behind her. He started slapping her on her back until she finally could speak and tell him to stop, that she was fine.

He walked over to the kitchen sink, grabbed the dishrag, and began mopping up the spill from the table. When Louise caught her breath, she reached for a handful of napkins and finished cleaning the mess. She stood up and walked over to the trash can and threw away the wet napkins. George wrung out the dishrag into the sink and hung it back over the faucet. He took in a deep breath and went back to his seat. Louise sat down again across from him.

"You okay?" he asked.

She nodded. "I don't think I heard you right," she noted, sitting forward in her seat and bracing her hands on the table.

George sat back in his seat as well. "No, I think you heard me exactly right," he responded. "I asked you to marry me."

He waited and then leaned in to Louise. "So, in case you choke again, I need to know, you want me to perform the Heimlich maneuver this time?"

Louise just shook her head and fell back in her chair.

Cocktail Meatballs

1 pound ground beef
2 tablespoons breadcrumbs
1 egg, slightly beaten
½ teaspoon salt
⅓ cup finely chopped onion
⅓ cup finely chopped green pepper
1 tablespoon butter
2 tablespoons brown sugar
1 can tomato soup
4 teaspoons Worcestershire sauce
1 tablespoon vinegar
1 tablespoon prepared mustard

Mix beef, crumbs, egg, and salt. Shape into 50 balls. Place in shallow baking pan. Broil until brown. Turn over. Spoon off fat. In saucepan, cook onion and pepper in butter until tender. Stir in remaining ingredients. Pour over meatballs. Cover and bake at 350 degrees for 20 minutes.

—Lester's Barbecue Shack

Chapter Five

"I don't understand." Jessie had ordered and handed the menu to the waitress. She and Louise and Bea were meeting for lunch. Bea was late, and Louise told Jessie the news before they even found their seats.

"I'll have the special and we'll have one more joining us. She wants the diet plate with pasta instead of the green salad and she wants her chicken fried instead of grilled."

The waitress looked at Louise with raised eyebrows and shook her head. "Is Beatrice on her way or do I need to hold the orders awhile?"

Louise smiled. The three of them had been regulars at Lester's Barbecue Shack for years. Nothing Beatrice did surprised any of the servers or cooks. There was the whole Christmas cake debacle in which she made promises about Lester making cakes that he never intended to make. Once she had even gone back to the kitchen to show the cook how to prepare her sandwich. She was known to be a fussy customer but she was loyal, and because of that, Lester didn't kick her out.

"Just wait a few minutes. Bea had to go to the bank before coming here so I don't know how long that will take. Just bring our drinks and when you see her, put our orders in." Louise handed her menu to the waitress.

"He asked me to marry him," Louise said to Jessie, who was still waiting for more information.

Jessie knew that George was visiting Louise, and she had been as curious as anybody about his reasons for coming to Hope Springs. "Has he lost his mind?" she asked, and then realized how harsh the question sounded. She waved her hand in front of her. "I didn't mean it like that, Lou. You would make a fine wife. I just meant, that, uh . . ." Jessie fumbled for words.

"I understand what you meant. I know because I asked him the same thing. What on earth would make him want to marry me?"

The waitress brought over three glasses of tea and set them before the women. Louise and Jessie both took a sip.

"But he's sick." Louise unwrapped a straw and stuck it in her glass.

"And he wants you to be his nurse?" Jessie asked. "That's degrading for him to ask of you."

Louise shook his head. "He's not asking for anything like that. He wants me to be his power of attorney, his health care proxy, and he wants me to get all of his money, all of his and Roxie's money, when he dies."

"Why wouldn't he want his girls to get anything?"

Louise dropped her hands in her lap. "Ruby married a loser who will gamble it away and Laura has too much money to care. I don't think either of them has much to do with George. I think they've been estranged since Roxie died."

Jessie waited. She was still trying to understand what this unexpected marriage proposal meant. "Well, what happened to the woman he left Roxie for? Why aren't they still married?"

"They never got married."

Jessie sighed. "So, I still don't get any of this. Did he suddenly realize after all of these years that he was actually madly in love with you?"

Louise laughed. "No, I don't think that's the reason behind this crazy notion."

"Then what?" Jessie asked again. "I just don't understand what made him drive all the way down here and ask this question if he didn't expect something in return from you." She glanced out the window. Beatrice was standing outside waving at the two of them. She waved back. "You hadn't heard from him in years, right?" Jessie asked.

"Right," Louise answered. She noticed Beatrice too. She looked over and got the attention of the waitress, who saw Beatrice as she walked in the front door.

The server reached into her pocket and pulled out the order ticket and placed it in line with the other tickets.

"I don't know really," Louise added. "He seems to think it's just karma or something. He was looking through old photo albums and remembering all of our old times together, me and him and Roxie, and he just decided that I was meant to have his inheritance, that Roxie would have wanted that. He seems to think us getting married would make amends to Roxie for his affair, for the fact that he left her."

"And he wants to marry you even though he knows you're not interested in . . ." Jessie cleared her throat, struggling to find the right words.

"Even though I'm gay?" Louise asked.

"It is kind of an important matter, don't you think?"

Louise waved at Beatrice as she started walking toward them. "I thought it was but he didn't seem to."

Jessie sighed and shook her head. The news from Louise had completely shocked her.

Beatrice made her way to the booth where the two friends were waiting. "I tell you what, if Dick Witherspoon wasn't my husband and we didn't have a joint account, I would take all of my money out of that bank and put it in a coffee can and bury it. We might as well be taking it down to the dog track as to let them keep investing it for us!" She huffed and sat down next to Jessie. She pulled the scarf from around her neck and placed it in her purse. "This one mine?" she asked, pointing to the third glass of tea.

Louise nodded. "Good afternoon, Bea," she

said. "Did you have a fight at the bank?" she asked.

"Some fight," Beatrice replied. "I told them to take my money out of their investment portfolio and give me a CD and a savings account. I'm tired of getting their loss statements every month." She smiled as she glanced over at Jessie and Louise. "But enough of that, hello friends," she said. "Did Jessie tell you about our wedding plans?"

Louise looked surprised.

"We hadn't gotten to that," Jessie responded. "There's been some other wedding news to talk about first." She glanced over to Louise, waiting for her to catch Beatrice up on the latest.

"Well, that certainly piques my interest. What wedding news?" Louise asked.

"Jessie and James are renewing their vows in May and we're calling Charlotte to come back and perform the ceremony. It's going to be in Jessie's backyard. We're going to have a nice reception with little finger foods, nothing over the top, but a little more dignified than chicken wings and potato chips, and a beautiful cake, of course. Casey Hampton is the photographer and his brother-in-law is making a video, which I guess now is really a DVD or some such as that. Sharon Newbright is handling the floral needs and Caroline Bender is going to sing a solo."

"Good heavens, Bea." Jessie turned to look at

her friend. "When on earth did you make all of those arrangements?" She shook her head in disbelief. "We only agreed to this thing a couple of days ago."

Beatrice drank a sip of her tea and pointed to the sugar packets. Louise slid the plastic holder over, and Beatrice pulled out three packets and poured them in her tea. "Why didn't you order sweet tea?" she asked.

Before either Jessie or Louise could answer that the tea was already sweetened, the waitress arrived with their lunches. She placed them in front of each of the women, calling out the order. When she got to Beatrice, she set the plate down on the table with the remark, "Diet plate," and rolled her eyes. Beatrice smiled and looked at her order. "No French fries?" she asked the server, who simply turned her head and walked away.

"What is with the attitude?" she asked her friends, who had already started to enjoy their food.

"It's supposed to be a diet plate," Louise replied. "And you turned it into the Hearty Man's Special."

Beatrice shrugged and reached for the salt and pepper. She seasoned her food and took her first bite.

"Well, Jessie, that is fabulous news about you and James. That will be a lovely event. And Charlotte is coming back for it?" Louise asked.

"I haven't called her yet," Beatrice explained.

The other two women looked at her in disbelief.

"You've arranged for a florist and a soloist and a photographer and you haven't called Charlotte to make sure she can make that date?" Jessie asked.

"And the videographer," Beatrice added. "And no, I tried Charlotte a couple of times yesterday and didn't reach her." She wiped her mouth and took a sip of tea. "Maria says her boyfriend was married before and didn't tell her. *No se puede confiar en los hombres.*" She shook her head. "Men are so untrustworthy," she translated. "So, I don't know what we are going to do about the police officer."

"What police officer?" Louise asked. She hadn't heard any of the recent news about their young friend. "And I didn't know you spoke Spanish."

"Sí," Beatrice responded with a grin.

"Oh, Charlotte is dating a young man in the Gallup Police Department and Beatrice is all upset because she wanted her to fall in love with a North Carolina boy. She even set her up with the funeral director's nephew."

"You set Charlotte up with Rollin Fair?" Louise asked. "Roly-poly Rollin?"

"He has not been called that since he was a teenager, Louise Fisher. He's almost forty years old now."

"And we still call him Roly-poly Rollin," Louise noted. She took another bite of her meat loaf.

"Beatrice found out that he was going to a conference in Albuquerque, so she decided to play matchmaker." Jessie reached for her tea. "I don't think it went so well," she added, taking a sip. She had also talked to Charlotte about her blind date.

"I thought he was married," Louise remarked. "I thought he married Jack and Rita's daughter from over in Winston-Salem."

Beatrice was enjoying her fried chicken. She nodded while she chewed. "She left him for her tennis instructor. This chicken is fried too hard," she commented.

"Well, I don't think you can send it back now." Louise was looking at Bea's plate, which was mostly empty.

Beatrice wiped her mouth. "You're probably right but somebody ought to tell Tony so that he can correct the problem," she noted as she ate the last bite of her chicken and then wiped her face and hands. "Okay, now Louise is caught up on Charlotte and the policeman." She placed her napkin beside her plate. "He's Indian, by the way," she added.

Louise nodded.

"And we're all on the same page about the wedding renewal in May, what else did I miss?"

Beatrice had finished her pasta and was starting on a dinner roll.

"Are we on the same page about the wedding renewal?" Jessie asked as she ate her sandwich.

Beatrice nodded while she cleaned her plate and reached for her tea. "Of course we are, Jessie."

"George Cannon is sick and he asked Louise to marry him," Jessie said.

Beatrice suddenly choked on her drink. She sputtered and coughed while Louise and Jessie gave her napkins and she tried to catch her breath again. Everyone in the diner turned to watch. Finally, she seemed okay.

"You know, I did the exact same thing. Made a mess on my blouse and all over the kitchen table," Louise noted.

Beatrice was taking in a few deep breaths. The two women waited for her response and to make sure that she was really fine. She held her hand on her chest. "I think this is so wonderful."

Jessie and Louise looked at each other. This was not at all the reaction they were expecting.

"You what?" Louise asked as the waitress came over and put more napkins on the table.

"Are you okay?" the waitress asked.

All three of them nodded.

"You want anything else?" she asked.

"Do you have any wedding cake?" Beatrice wanted to know.

The server seemed confused. "We still have a few slices of chocolate cake but I don't think it's for anybody's wedding."

"Well, it is now!" Beatrice announced. "Let us have one slice and three forks." The waitress walked over to the counter and took out the chocolate cake.

"Why are you happy about this?" Louise asked, surprised at Bea.

"Who doesn't love a wedding?" Beatrice asked. "And I need more tea." She turned and yelled at the waitress, "And make this batch sweet!" She glanced around at her friends. "You need more tea?" she asked.

Jessie and Louise shook their heads, still stunned at the response from Beatrice. She didn't even ask any questions.

"Bea, Louise doesn't even like George. He had an affair while he was married to her best friend, when she was dying." Jessie was staring at Beatrice.

"Not to mention that I'm not that thrilled about the idea of living with a man," Louise added. She waited while Beatrice took the dessert plate from the waitress, had more tea poured in her glass, and positioned the plate in the center of the table. The server handed out the forks.

"Have you forgotten who I am?" Louise finally asked.

"You're Louise Fisher, fabulous friend to Jessie

and me and Margaret and Roxie Barnett Cannon. You're a terrific gardener, especially with those little bonsai trees, and an excellent typist. You're a terrible cook but you still participate in the potlucks at church by bringing simple salads or cookies you buy from Sam's Club. You do make good iced tea. You're very smart with crossword puzzles and you haven't bought a new sweater in ten years."

Louise glanced down at her sweater.

Beatrice continued. "You send a small donation every month to the Humane Society because deep down you think animals are much closer to God than people. You're very smart, read a lot of historical fiction, and you're all paid up on your funeral costs."

Louise set down her fork and stared at Beatrice.

Beatrice took a bite of cake, chewed, and swallowed. She smiled. "And George Cannon owes you for taking care of his wife, so you marry him, let him take care of your household needs, pay your bills, and then when he dies, you get all of Roxie's things and all of his life insurance and Social Security." She took another bite of cake. "This is really good," she said. "How much money does he have, by the way?"

"I don't know," Louise replied. "I wouldn't imagine there's a lot. He and Roxie never lived a life of luxury. But really, that's of no interest to me."

"Well, it should be, and you should find that out before you jump in his bed," Bea responded.

Jessie took a bite of cake. She had nothing to add to Beatrice's line of reasoning.

"But aren't you forgetting something?" Louise asked, still astonished at her friend.

"What?" Bea asked. "Oh, the wedding," she noted, and then put down her fork. "Hey, why don't we do a double ceremony with James and Jessie?" She clapped her hands together at such a great idea. "We will already have all the necessary flourishes and attendants! It would be perfect!"

"No, I'm not talking about the wedding ceremony," Louise said. "I'm talking about the fact that I don't love George Cannon. I thought you were the great romantic. Shouldn't two people love each other when they get married?" she asked.

Jessie nodded. She thought what Louise was saying made perfect sense.

Beatrice made a kind of shooshing noise and waved the idea away. "Love?" she asked. "I'm with Tina Turner on this one," she added. The other two women looked confused. "You didn't see that movie about her and Ike?"

The two friends shook their heads.

"What has love got to do with it?" she asked.

Louise shook her head. "Aren't you even curious as to why he drove down here to ask me?"

Beatrice shrugged. "Not really," she responded. "I suppose it was what, guilt? Loneliness? The need for a companion? He's dying and doesn't want his children to make decisions for him?" She took the last bite of cake. "Does it really matter?"

"I would say that yes, it matters quite a lot." Jessie had finally chimed in. She was stunned to hear that Beatrice seemed to know so much without hearing the entire story. "Louise shouldn't enter into a marriage with a man she doesn't love. Louise is gay. She'd be selling out to marry a man."

Beatrice looked over at Jessie, then turned to Louise. "So what, that she's gay? Haven't most gay people our age been married to a straight person at some point in their lives? And furthermore, do you think Louise is ever going to look for a woman to love? Do you think she shouldn't get married because she's waiting for the perfect woman?" She waited. Neither woman replied.

"I rest my case."

"Well, even if I wasn't going to try to find a companion for myself, somebody I could really love, I don't think that means I should settle for somebody I would never pick, somebody I don't love."

"George loved Roxie. You loved Roxie, and Roxie loved both of you. I think that's enough of a foundation for a marriage right there. The love you shared for the same woman makes you somehow connected. So why not renew the friendship you had at one time with George and find out why Roxie loved him? Maybe you'll find something there that gives you a little bit of joy. At the very least, you'd feel closer to the one woman you have loved. And after all, she would want you to have her stuff." Beatrice took a sip of her tea and pointed again to the sugar.

Jessie reached over and took out three packets. She shook her head again as she handed them to Beatrice. "I don't agree with you, Beatrice. Louise deserves to have real love in her life as much as anyone. I don't think she should settle for anything less in a relationship. This just doesn't seem right."

"I don't disagree with you, Jessie," Beatrice noted, pouring the sugar into her glass of iced tea. "But Louise isn't ever going to pursue someone to love. So why not take the full benefits that you and I get in our marriages from somebody who has pursued her?" She looked over at Louise. "You can't tell me that you haven't really considered this. Otherwise you would have sent George packing as soon as he asked and you'd be laughing about this whole thing instead of telling us about it as if you're looking for an answer." She took a sip. "So tell Jessie the truth. You have really thought about it, haven't you?"

Jessie looked at Louise and waited for an answer but Louise simply hesitated and, shaking her head, just glanced away.

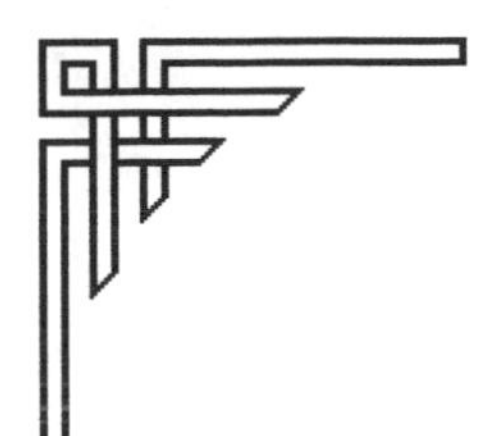

Party Mix

½ pound salted Spanish peanuts
½ pound salted nuts
3¾ cups slim pretzels
3 cups bite-size shredded wheat squares
5½ cups doughnut-shaped oat cereal
4 cups bite-size rice cereal squares
½ pound butter, melted
1 tablespoon Worcestershire sauce
1½ teaspoons garlic salt
1½ teaspoons salt

Combine peanuts, nuts, pretzels, and cereals in a large roaster. Add melted butter, Worcestershire sauce, garlic salt, and salt. Mix together thoroughly. Bake at 250 degrees for 2 hours, stirring gently with a wooden spoon every 15 minutes. Store in sealed, air-tight jars. Makes 4 quarts.

—Charlotte Stewart

Chapter Six

The phone call from Officer Donovan Sanchez to St. Mary's women's shelter was not a social call. Maria answered the phone and immediately transferred it to Charlotte. Just by the tone of his voice, by the way he asked to speak to the executive director, Maria could tell this was entirely business. She didn't know for sure what the Gallup Police Department was doing calling the shelter but she had her ideas, and she knew it wasn't about a police officer asking someone to go out on a date. She got up from her desk to listen because she knew arrangements were going to need to be made for another battered woman being referred to the shelter.

"Charlotte Stewart speaking." Charlotte was working at her desk, trying to finish the end-of-the-month reports. They were due in a couple of days and she was pushing to meet the deadline.

"It's Donovan," and he paused for only a second. "We have a victim here at the station. She's pretty messed up but she won't go to the hospital. You got room?"

"Of course," Charlotte answered, surprised to hear from Donovan and with such a professional request. It wasn't unusual to hear from the Gallup police, but generally one of the female officers assigned to follow up domestic abuse cases called. She had never dealt with Donovan professionally but she was glad to hear his voice even if it was business. "And I'll contact our on-call nurse to see if she can come by to check her out," she added.

"You going to be there in an hour?" he asked.

Charlotte saw the clock. It was almost five P.M. "Yeah, I'll probably be here all night," she replied. "Are you bringing her?"

"I am now," he responded.

Charlotte couldn't help herself, even with the news of another battered woman coming to the shelter; she smiled. Officer Sanchez was definitely making an impact on her. "Then I'll see you soon."

"Yep, I need to fill out some reports and assign another officer to go and pick up the husband, the perpetrator," he added, "but we should be there in about an hour."

"We'll be ready," Charlotte noted, and then asked, "What's her name?"

"Carla Fairhope," he replied.

Charlotte waited for a second, thinking that the name sounded vaguely familiar.

"Carla Sanchez Fairhope," he added, and Charlotte sat up in her chair.

There was a pause in the conversation.

"It's my ex-wife."

Charlotte was at a loss for words. She looked up and saw Maria was standing in the doorway. She wasn't sure how much the other woman had heard.

"I'll explain when I get there," he said, his voice softer than before.

"Okay," she said. "I'll see you soon."

"Thanks," Donovan said, and hung up the phone.

"Señor ten piedad!" Maria was making the sign of the cross. She put down her hands and waited for instructions.

"We have another resident coming. Donovan—" She stopped. "Officer Sanchez," Charlotte said, opting for a more professional tone, "will be bringing her in about an hour. He said that she was in pretty bad shape but that she won't go to the hospital. So call Laurie and ask if she can come over to check her out."

Maria nodded and turned around to go and make the call to one of the nurses who volunteered her services to the shelter.

"Wait, Maria, there's something else." Charlotte stopped her.

Maria turned back to face Charlotte. She waited for the additional instructions. She wondered if there were children coming as well and whether they had room for a family.

"It's somebody you know," Charlotte said.

Maria crossed herself again and braced herself for the news.

"It's Carla Fairhope," she announced. "Carla Sanchez Fairhope."

Maria shook her head as if she was unsure of the name, and then she immediately recognized it.

"Is this going to be okay for you?" Charlotte asked. She knew that Maria knew the family but she wasn't really sure how close they were.

Maria was still surprised by the news. She shook her head. "I don't know the Fairhopes," she said. "I know Isabella and Daniel. I don't know Daniel's family."

Charlotte nodded. She thought she remembered the line of family members that Maria had mentioned a week or so earlier but she wasn't sure. She also understood that Maria knew a number of the clients who came to St. Mary's, so that really wasn't the main issue. She was concerned mostly because they both now understood that this was Charlotte's new boyfriend's ex-wife.

Charlotte never worried about the issue of confidentiality with her number one volunteer. Maria had never divulged names of clients or ever spoken to anyone about who was staying at St. Mary's. She understood that not only were the identities of the residents not to be shared, but neither was the location of the shelter. Maria never even told anybody that she volunteered there. So Charlotte wasn't concerned about Maria telling anyone that Carla Fairhope was checking in, but she did think that Maria needed to know who was coming and to decide whether she wanted to be there when Carla arrived.

"I have no business in your relationships. A woman has been beaten, and she needs shelter and care and protection. That is all I intend to provide her when she comes." Maria appeared very serious.

Charlotte nodded in return and Maria left to make the necessary calls. Charlotte made her way to the bedrooms in the back of the house. Two of the residents were busy cleaning.

"We have somebody else joining us," Charlotte reported.

The two women turned to Charlotte.

Iris, an older woman, still recovering from the bruises she received two weeks earlier from her grandson, shook her head. "Jesus Almighty, how many of us are there out there?" she asked.

"More than you'll ever hear about," Darlene replied. She was younger than Iris, about forty, and had just escaped from her second abusive marriage. She had been at the shelter for six months and was still trying to find a new place to live.

"Can you help me make the spare bed in your room, Iris?" Charlotte asked. It was unusual for the shelter since they were almost always full to capacity, but on that particular day they actually had an available bed. Earlier that week, they had enjoyed a good-bye party for a previous resident named Lois and her two children. Lois was one of the lucky ones and could stay in the area. Her abusive boyfriend had been sentenced to a number of years in prison, and Lois had found a job at the casino in Sky City and a place to live just on the outskirts of the pueblo.

Iris had been in the room by herself only a couple of nights but she, like all of the other residents, knew resources at St. Mary's were to be shared. There were always more women in need than there was space, but the residents, glad to be safe, never complained.

"There are still two drawers empty too," Iris said. "And if she needs more, I can move my stuff under the bed."

"I don't think our newest resident has much stuff," Charlotte responded. "She's coming from the police station, and the officer said she was pretty messed up." Charlotte sighed. "So she probably just ran for her life, and you know what that means."

"She ain't got nothing but the clothes on her back," Darlene answered.

Charlotte nodded, and Iris shook her head, making a kind of *tsk tsk tsk* sound.

"I just can't believe that this kind of thing happens like it does. My husband never laid a hand on me, not in forty-three years of marriage, and I will never understand what happened to my grandson that made him snap like he did." Iris reached up and touched the bruise that was still visible above her eye. She had required twelve stitches to sew up the gash that had been the result of being hit by a baseball bat. Her grandson was twenty, still living at home, and had been charged with assault and battery and drug possession. She was brought to St. Mary's because her daughter and son-in-law said that they couldn't keep her and their other two children. She had nowhere else to go when she was released from the hospital. Charlotte was trying to help Iris find suitable housing at a retirement home, but she wanted to get the older woman healed up before moving her into her own apartment.

"Your grandson was on crack," Darlene noted, remembering her housemate's story when she arrived. "Drugs will make a person violent and crazy." She shook her head. "I should know because I been on both ends of that kind of violence." Darlene was a recovering addict. She had been in and out of group homes, halfway houses, and women's shelters since she left home at sixteen. But she was proud of herself because she celebrated ten years of sobriety and being clean. She and her second husband had quit drugs at the same time, and she always thought his violent streak had to do with his use of cocaine. She almost died the last time he threw her down the stairs at the apartment where they lived, and after that last time, she finally quit making excuses for him and moved into the shelter.

"Well, let's try and get this bed made, and, Iris, the nurse is coming to have a look at our newest guest, so you may need to let them have the room until after dinner. And then she may need a little time alone." Charlotte glanced at her watch. She was trying to remember what else she needed to do before Carla's arrival.

"We'll take care of it, Sister Charlotte. You go do your executive director work. We'll make the bed and clean up a little in that room." Darlene winked and nodded.

Most of the women called Charlotte "Sister Charlotte" because the majority of them had never met a woman minister, and it was just easier to identify her as a nun. Charlotte never corrected them because she actually enjoyed being called "Sister." It made her feel connected to the women as more than just an executive director or social worker. It made her feel like family.

"Thanks, Darlene," Charlotte responded. She turned and walked back to her office. She wanted to make sure that Maria had gotten hold of the nurse and that she was going to be able to stop by.

Maria met her in the doorway to the office. "Laurie said she can be here in an hour," she reported.

"Great," Charlotte said. She moved over to her desk and sat down.

"Did he tell you who she was?" Maria asked.

Charlotte nodded. She knew that Maria was asking about Donovan and referring to the relationship between him and the victim, not just the woman's name. "He told me she was his ex-wife," she replied.

"Is he in any danger?" Maria asked.

Charlotte looked up at the volunteer. She hadn't even considered that. Surely, she thought, the abuser knew his wife's ex-husband. He probably even had guessed that he would be the person she ran to. What if he went looking for Donovan before the police could pick him up? she wondered. "I don't know," she answered. "He was sending another officer to make the arrest."

Maria paused. "He's bringing her here then?" she asked.

Charlotte nodded.

"You need me to do anything else before they come?" she asked.

Charlotte considered the question. "We'll probably need some medical supplies. Can you get the first aid kit from the storage room? The big one," she added, "the one with the large bandages. And we should probably get towels and some of the old sheets to put over the bed linens."

"We don't know what kind of injuries she has?" Maria asked.

Charlotte shook her head. "Donovan just said that she was pretty messed up and that she should go to the hospital."

Maria considered this information. "I'll get the Ace bandages from the laundry room." She had just washed a large stack of them earlier in the day.

The shelter went through lots of Ace bandages. There were always sprains and broken bones healing at St. Mary's. "How about dinner for the others?" she asked.

"It's Iris's turn to cook and the groceries were picked up yesterday, so she'll take care of that after she and Darlene have cleaned up," Charlotte replied. "Oh, I knew I needed to be somewhere." She shook her head, recalling a previously arranged engagement.

"What?" Maria asked.

"I need to get Martha and Denise from the bus depot." She remembered that two of the residents were waiting to be picked up after their day of work, and then she was supposed to pick up Martha's two children from a day care center not too far away from the depot. She glanced at her watch. She had been planning to pick them up, get the children, and then stop by a local parish to get supplies they had collected during the holidays. She had been trying to get there to pick the supplies up for weeks and just hadn't found the opportunity. She had forgotten until just at that moment that she had made arrangements to pick things up that evening.

Maria seemed to read Charlotte's mind. "I can get Gilbert to go to that church," she noted. "He knows exactly where it is and he has a truck," she volunteered. "And I'll go get the girls."

Charlotte smiled. "You are the best!"

"Can I wait at least to see how you look at each other when he gets here with his ex-wife?" Maria asked.

Charlotte laughed. "No, because Martha and Denise will freeze out there waiting for you if you do."

Maria nodded. "Yes, it's true. It is cold out there. I will leave now to collect them."

Charlotte was actually glad that Maria wasn't going to be around when Donovan showed up. She knew it was going to be awkward. Here was *her* date bringing *his ex-wife* to the battered women's shelter where *she* worked. She wasn't sure what to expect, but she would rather face it alone than have her friend watching his every move and then making judgments about what she thought she was seeing.

"This may be a sign," Maria said as she gathered her coat and gloves and looked around for the keys to the van.

"What kind of sign?" Charlotte asked, seeing the keys on the edge of her desk. She picked them up and was getting ready to toss them to Maria.

"The kind that says, *Peligro! Ese hombre no es para ti!*"

Charlotte shook her head and pitched the keys to Maria. She was able to translate this because she had heard it from her friend a hundred times. It was the same thing Maria told every woman to say to herself once she was discharged from St. Mary's and was thinking about dating again too soon. She had told Lois this only a few days earlier.

"Danger ahead! That man is not for you!"

Cheese Pennies

2 cups grated cheddar cheese
1 stick margarine
1 cup flour
1 teaspoon salt
1¼ teaspoons red pepper

Cream cheese and margarine. Mix flour, salt, and pepper. Add to cheese and mix well. Roll in sticks. Wrap in waxed paper. Chill 30 minutes. Slice thin. Bake 15 minutes at 350 degrees. Place on crackers.

—Iris T.

Chapter Seven

Charlotte was in the kitchen, helping Iris toss a salad, when Donovan arrived with Carla. She saw the headlights of the patrol car as they pulled into the driveway. She put down the knife she was using to slice tomatoes and wiped her hands on the front of her pants. "Can you finish fixing supper?" she asked Iris.

"Of course," Iris replied. "You go on and conduct your business, Sister Charlotte."

Charlotte smiled. "Maria will be back soon with Martha and Denise and the children. So you all go ahead and eat. Don't wait for us. I sort of doubt our new resident will be dining with us anyway."

Iris glanced toward the clock. It was just before six. "Yes, Sister," she responded, and then went back to her food preparation.

Charlotte took in a deep breath. Receiving new clients was always hard for her. The endless line of abused and broken women, the scared and brutalized children clutching the backs of their mother's legs, the fear and the unnecessary shame, it was all so overwhelming to the executive director. The arrivals were always the hardest part.

Charlotte had been a parish minister before taking this job, and she had seen some heartbreaking things in that position. She had sat at deathbeds and been in emergency waiting rooms to hear of horrible wrecks and unsuspected illnesses. She had visited prisons and been in homes where sorrow was a regular guest. She had dealt with anger and sadness and grief as heavy as clouds. She had fought battles and lost wars and been so dog-tired that she would sometimes stand in the pulpit without a word of comfort or kindness. But nothing in that line of work ever prepared her for the depth of the pain and agony and the level of desperation she experienced at St. Mary's.

Every woman was unique. Every woman had a story that was unique. And yet the fundamentals were always the same. The woman had left an abusive relationship. She had nothing but what she was wearing or what she could carry. She had no idea of what she was going to do beyond run for her safety and get out of her relationship. After that was when the women and their stories diverged. After those basic facts, the women and how they handled their situations were as different and as unpredictable as storms in winter.

Some of the women made it, finding new housing, finding new employment, being able to make a real break from their abusers and their abusive lives. They were the success stories. They were the ones Charlotte spoke of when she gave her report at the board of directors' meetings. They were the ones she recited to herself over and over, and especially when she found herself feeling defeated and despairing. The success stories were what kept her going, and kept her at St. Mary's.

Many of the women, on the other hand, didn't make it. A lot of the women went back to their former lives, simply unable to imagine any other way of life for themselves. They went back into the arms of their tormentors and back into a violent cycle that eventually, one way or another, killed them. That aspect of her work, that choice of destruction that was often taken, that decision to go back to a violent way of life, those stories, those and the children, were the hardest parts of the job.

No matter how long she worked at St. Mary's, the way the children cowered and played in silence, the way they flinched if someone came too close, the tiny ways violence broke them, that was something Charlotte could never get used to. She looked for signs of hope, possibilities for change, but no matter how she learned to deal with domestic abuse, she could never find a way to be resigned to what happened to the children.

She slid her shoulder-length hair behind her ears and stopped in the hallway bathroom to take a quick look in the mirror before moving to the front door. Usually not a woman who cared too much about her appearance, since meeting Donovan she found herself applying a little more makeup in the mornings and taking a bit more interest in the clothes she decided to wear. This whole new way of being, of thinking about how she looked, was foreign to her, but so were the feelings she had for the Gallup police officer.

She was in the hallway just as the doorbell rang, and she opened the door and stood just inside the landing. Donovan was in front and a woman, one she couldn't yet see, stood behind him in the shadows.

"Hey," Donovan said as he dipped his head at Charlotte. He was wearing his uniform, minus the hat, which was securely placed beneath his left arm, which was at his side, while the other rested across his chest.

Charlotte had never seen him in his uniform. When they first met, when her car had a flat tire and he stopped to help, he was off duty and was wearing jeans and a sweatshirt. When they went out for the one date they shared, he was in his civilian clothes as well. She was surprised at how authoritative he looked standing in front of her in the standard Gallup police uniform.

"Hello," she responded, and stepped aside so that the two of them could walk in.

Donovan moved inside and the woman followed him. Charlotte could not get a very good look at her even in the light because she kept her shoulders hunched over and her head to the ground. Once she was in, Charlotte closed the door behind them, and they stood in the landing for a few awkward moments.

"Carla, this is Charlotte. This is the woman I've

told you about, and this is St. Mary's." He spoke softly.

"Hello, Carla," Charlotte chimed in. "It's nice to meet you," she added, holding out her hand to shake.

Carla reached her hand out, and immediately Charlotte noticed the large bruises around her wrist. She had seen marks like that before. It usually meant the perpetrator had held the woman down. It usually was a sign that a rape had occurred. It appeared as if her thumb, swollen and blue, was broken. Charlotte shook the extended hand carefully. The woman didn't speak but she did look up, and Charlotte tried not to react to the terrible markings on her face.

Both of her eyes were swollen shut. Her bottom lip was split and had been bleeding. Her nose had been smashed. Everything on her face was cut or bruised, and it was easy to see why Donovan had said that she needed to be at a hospital.

"Oh my." Charlotte sighed, trying not to react too strongly. She shook her head. "You're going to need a couple of stitches on that lip," she noted. "Are you in a lot of pain?" she asked.

Carla shook her head slightly. It was obvious that more than a slight movement hurt a great deal.

"Laurie, our nurse on staff, will be here soon and she'll take a good look at you, and we'll do what we can for your injuries here. But you may need an

X-ray of your nose and cheeks." Charlotte had gotten very good at her initial assessments of battered women. She had learned who needed medical attention and even what tests would be appropriate.

Carla shook her head again and dropped her face.

"Her husband works at the hospital," Donovan said. "She won't go because she's afraid he'll find out where she is."

Charlotte nodded. "We can take her down to Grants to the clinic there or even to Albuquerque, if we need to." She had run into this problem before and taken women to hospitals or medical facilities out of town. Often the abuser knew the damage he had done, and if the victim wouldn't press charges or if the police couldn't find him, the hospital in Gallup was not a safe option.

Carla shook her head again. "Nothing's broken," she said. "Except maybe a couple of ribs, and there really isn't anything they do for those anyway," she added.

"Carla is a nurse tech," Donovan explained.

Charlotte smiled. "Okay," she responded. "No hospitals or urgent care facilities. But you will let Laurie, our nurse, take a look, won't you?"

Carla nodded and lowered her head again.

"What would you like to do right now?" Charlotte asked. "Would you like to wash up a bit or lie down? Or if you're hungry, we can fix you a plate for supper."

There was a pause. Carla seemed to be trying to figure out what she wanted most at that moment. Charlotte waited for her to respond.

"I think I'd like to take a shower," she answered. "Yes, I'd just like to take a shower," she convinced herself.

Charlotte nodded. "It's helpful, Carla, if we take some pictures of your injuries. I know it's a terrible thing to do, but we've found that having these photographs when you first come in, as evidence of the crime, it's just helpful." She tried to make the request as easy and kind as she could. She hated this part of the intake procedure, but she had found over the years that by the time court cases rolled around, judges and lawyers had a difficult time believing the extent of injuries without photographic evidence.

Carla glanced up at Donovan.

"We did that already," he replied, speaking for her. "One of the women officers took them," he explained. "Since she came to the station, we had to file a report, and so it's just standard procedure to take pictures."

"Good," Charlotte noted. "So, now you can take your shower." She gestured toward the hallway and escorted Carla to the bathroom. She pulled out a towel and cloth from the pantry and handed them to Carla. She showed her where the soap and shampoo and lotion were. She explained the hot and cold water and how she needed to be careful because the hot water could get very hot. She also found a pair of sweatpants and a sweatshirt, a new pair of underwear and socks, and handed them to Carla. The newest resident of St. Mary's glanced down at the clothes.

"We have a lot of new and used clothes here," Charlotte said. "Most of our residents don't have anything when they come. You're welcome to use whatever you need. The clothes are in the bins and hanging on the racks in the back room." She gestured down the hall.

Carla nodded. "Thank you," she said softly.

"You're welcome," Charlotte replied. "Take as long as you need." And she closed the bathroom door and headed back up the hall.

Donovan was still standing near the front door. By this time, Maria and the other women had come in the back door, but out of respect and because of their recollections of their own arrivals at the shelter, none of them had come into the front room. Even Maria had not come in the front area. She had just gone into the kitchen, grabbed a dinner roll, and left. Charlotte was surprised to find out later that her volunteer had not stepped inside to meet Donovan.

"You want to sit down for a minute?" Charlotte asked Donovan as she walked back into the room. She could hear the women talking quietly in the kitchen and dining room.

"Sure," he replied. And he took a seat on the sofa

while Charlotte sat across from him in one of the overstuffed chairs.

"She was beaten pretty bad," Charlotte commented.

Donovan nodded.

"I'm glad she felt like she could come to you," she added.

Donovan nodded again. He seemed embarrassed about the situation.

"He's hit her before," he responded. "But never like this," he added. He shook his head and slid his hat in his lap. He fingered the edges and then glanced up at Charlotte.

Charlotte didn't respond.

"We've been divorced eighteen years," he explained. "We got married right out of high school. We were young, stupid. And we lasted about six years when she realized she didn't want to be married to a cop and I realized that she was still interested in being young and, well, stupid." He paused. "Carla has always been a bit on the wild side," he added. "I'm more, well, I'm a little on the boring side." He managed a smile.

Charlotte nodded and returned the smile. "But you've stayed friends?" she asked.

Donovan shook his head. "Not really," he replied. "She tends to show up when she's in trouble," he added. "It's not usually this kind of trouble." He shrugged. "Money, usually. She's come to me from time to time because she's needed money."

Charlotte settled into her seat. She studied Donovan. He was a big man, broad shoulders, stocky and yet still tall. He had dark hair and eyes, and skin that was brown, like he stayed in the sun all day. He seemed nervous, and Charlotte understood that this was uncomfortable for him.

"Do you know her husband?" she asked.

"I know of him," Donovan replied. "He's been in trouble before. He's known to have a violent streak."

Charlotte nodded.

"A few bar brawls, a bunch of skirmishes with some other drunks. A few arrests. I tried to tell Carla before she married him but she wouldn't listen."

"How long have they been married?" Charlotte wanted to know.

"About six years," Donovan answered.

"And there's somebody out looking for him?" Charlotte asked, wondering if the other police officers had succeeded yet.

"We sent a unit over to their house. I suspect he's still there."

"Why?" Charlotte asked.

"Carla got one good swing at him before she ran out," Donovan replied.

"She doesn't look like she could do much damage," Charlotte noted. "She's very petite," she added, thinking about the small woman she had just met.

"She had an iron skillet," Donovan said with a slight smile.

"Well, that does help if you don't match up," Charlotte responded.

"She said he was knocked out when she left."

Charlotte nodded. She knew that some of the battered women she met were able to fight back. Some of them were quite strong and could hold their own in a fistfight. Some of the others, most of them, in fact, were generally too scared and too weak. Charlotte had noticed that violent men seemed to be drawn to the smaller, meeker types.

There was a pause in the conversation. They could hear the women talking and eating in the dining room. There was some laughter, which always made Charlotte smile. There was not usually a lot of laughter at St. Mary's.

"Thank you for taking her," Donovan finally broke the silence. "I didn't know where else for her to go."

"That's why we're here," Charlotte responded. "You know, it's funny that we've never met before," she added. "I know most of the police officers in Gallup." She thought about all of the men and women she had met in her line of work. She knew all the emergency room staff at the hospital, many of the local clergy, social workers, school counselors, police officers, and, unfortunately, funeral directors. When she discovered that Donovan served on the force in Gallup, she had been surprised to find out that he had never brought a woman to St. Mary's.

Donovan nodded. He wasn't sure why he had never come to the women's shelter. He had certainly handled domestic violence calls, but in his experience, most of the women wouldn't leave their homes.

There was another pause. "I'm sorry I didn't tell you that I was married before," he finally confessed. "I wasn't hiding it," he added. "I just didn't tell you."

"We've only been out once," Charlotte noted. "We hadn't really had the chance to go into a lot of detail about our lives."

"You don't count the tire change as a first date?" he asked.

Charlotte grinned. "Well, there was a little more to it than just roadside assistance, wasn't there?"

"Coffee," he replied. "And we did talk awhile that night," he added.

Charlotte blushed even though she wasn't sure why. She glanced away from Donovan and cleared her throat. "So, does Carla have family she can go to when she's stronger?" she asked.

Realizing that the conversation had changed directions, he answered the question. "She has a couple of sisters and her mother is still living. I suppose I should let them know what has happened," he said.

"I'd let her make that decision," Charlotte advised.

They both noticed the lights of the car pulling into the driveway of the house.

"That's probably the nurse," Charlotte guessed. "I better go meet her at the back and tell her what to expect."

Donovan stood up, understanding it was his cue to leave. "Thank you again," he said. "Can I call tomorrow?" he asked.

Charlotte wasn't sure whether he meant her or the shelter for Carla but she answered positively regardless. "Of course." She thought for a moment. "I did give you my card, right?" she asked.

Donovan smiled and pulled it out from the front of his shirt pocket. "Reverend Charlotte Stewart," he read. "Call me day or night," he added.

"It doesn't say that," Charlotte responded, knowing that he was teasing her.

"No, but it probably should," he said. He stuck the card back where it had been and headed for the door. "You'd take a call anytime, wouldn't you?"

She nodded. "Probably," she replied.

"I'll call tomorrow," he said.

"We'll be here," Charlotte replied, still unsure whom he was intending to talk to.

She opened the door and he headed down the steps, and when Charlotte turned around, the women from the shelter were all gathered in the hallway watching.

Clam Dip

1 6½-ounce can minced clams
1½ cups sour cream
1 teaspoon onion salt
¼ teaspoon salt
¼ teaspoon Worcestershire sauce

Drain clams; reserve 2 tablespoons liquid. Combine clams, reserved liquid, and remaining ingredients. Chill 3 to 4 hours. Serve with crackers. Makes 2 ½ cups.

—Eldon Macintyre

Chapter Eight

Beatrice saw the mailman as he rounded the corner. She threw on her coat and met him at her front gate just as he was about to bring the mail to her box on her front porch. "Eldon," she said, studying the man who had delivered her mail for almost twenty years.

"Mrs. Witherspoon," he acknowledged. "How are you today?" he asked.

"I'm as perky as a peach," she replied. "And how are you?"

He handed her a small stack of letters. "I am fine."

She took the stack and kept watching the man. "How is Lily?" she asked, sounding as if she knew the answer.

"Lily is fine." Eldon appeared as if he really wasn't interested in a conversation. "Have a good day now." And he turned to walk away.

Beatrice stopped him. "Eldon," she called out before he had taken a step.

He turned back around. "Yes, Mrs. Witherspoon?"

"This spring Jessie and James Jenkins are renewing their vows. The *Farmers' Almanac* reports that the weather this year will be particularly kind for outdoor events, and I think it's high time you marry that woman." Beatrice was needling Eldon to propose to the woman he had been dating for as long as he had been a mailman. For fifteen years she had pestered him about his lack of commitment.

Eldon sighed a heavy sigh. "Beatrice," he said, remembering that the older woman had told him years ago to call her by her first name, "Lily broke up with me about nine months ago. I didn't tell you like I didn't tell anybody because I can't stand the questions and the look of pity that is starting to form on your face right now."

Beatrice tried to change her expression. She could feel the pity look when it started to emerge.

Eldon continued. "She's found somebody new and she's happy. So don't ask me anymore about her. Don't tell me to marry her. Don't talk to me about Lily Bitterman ever again." He turned away from Beatrice and looked up the street. "I've got a route to make, and besides, it looks like you have received an important wedding invitation to attend to, so with that announcement postmarked from Columbia, South Carolina, and the Jenkins one, I'd say you got plenty of nuptials to keep you busy this spring." And he tipped his hat at Beatrice and headed down the sidewalk.

"Well, Eldon Macintyre, why on earth wouldn't you think you could tell me about your breakup? I mean nothing but goodwill for you." Beatrice kept talking but Eldon never turned around. "I'll find you a woman, Eldon!" she yelled, and it was loud enough that a couple of neighbors who were standing outside turned to look in her direction.

Beatrice smiled at them and waved. She never was one to worry about what others thought of her. She headed back to the house and glanced down at her stack of letters. On top was indeed what appeared to be a wedding invitation. She looked back up the street at Eldon as he moved in and out of driveways, delivering the mail. It surprised her to hear that he had noticed her letters. He had always seemed so discreet, acting as if he never paid any attention at all to anybody's mail.

Beatrice studied the letter and suddenly noticed the return address, and she recognized it as her daughter Robin's address in Columbia, South Carolina. The envelope was a thick paper stock, expensive, Beatrice could tell. It was mauve in color, with a gold-stamped pair of wedding rings on the back.

Robin had moved from Charlotte, North Carolina, a few years earlier. She was a banker, a loan officer, and she had gotten a promotion that involved a move south. It hadn't seemed like such a big deal for Beatrice because she rarely saw any of her children anyway, and Robin especially seemed always too busy to come back to Hope Springs to visit her mother and stepfather. As far as Beatrice knew, Robin had not been dating anyone and was a very committed single woman. Beatrice had given up on matchmaking for her daughter after she graduated from college. But it was certainly not because she lost heart. Her resignation came entirely from Robin, who claimed that if her mother didn't quit setting her up on blind dates or giving out her phone number to young men, she was going to take a job in San Francisco, and never speak to Beatrice again. Her mother got the message loud and clear and never tried matchmaking on her again. Still, she always asked about Robin's love life, and she had never heard Robin mention anyone that she was dating.

Beatrice held the invitation carefully as she walked to the front steps of her house. She sat down on the top step and slowly opened it. She pulled out the card and as she read the words, she couldn't believe it. It was exactly as it appeared. Robin was getting married, and Beatrice was finding out from a wedding invitation. It read:

Robin Newgarden

and

Farrell Monk

Invite you to their

Destination wedding.

July 3, 2010
2:00 P.M.
Cabo San Lucas, Mexico

That was it. Inside the envelope there was also a short letter of explanation about how to reserve airline tickets and rooms at the hotel, an itinerary of events that lasted the entire weekend, and a phone number to call for more information and to RSVP.

Beatrice stared at the invitation. She shook her head, trying to understand how her own daughter could be getting married and she had not known that she was even dating. All kinds of questions rolled across her mind. *Who was Farrell Monk? How long had they known each other? Why hadn't she told her mother anything about the relationship? Why hadn't Beatrice met her future son-in-law? And where was Cabo San Lucas and why would Robin choose to get married in another country instead of in her hometown?*

Beatrice was not even able to name all the emotions she was feeling. There was betrayal and disappointment, but mostly there was just hurt. She and Robin had certainly gone through hard times together. They started fighting when Robin was a baby, and the fights never seemed to stop. But Beatrice thought they had moved beyond that. She thought they were closer now that Robin was an adult. They had not had a disagreement in years. Beatrice would have never imagined that her daughter could leave her out of something so important as her wedding, as the event of falling in love, even the engagement. Beatrice sat with her head in her hands, the invitation fallen at her feet, and began to cry. She was so lost in her sorrow that she didn't even hear Eldon Macintyre, the mailman, as he walked up and stood in front of her.

"I came to say I was sorry," he said, surprised to see Beatrice in tears.

There was no reply.

"Are you okay, Mrs. Witherspoon?" It was clear that she wasn't, and he was suddenly awkward and embarrassed that he had returned to her house.

"Did you know about this?" she asked.

"What?" Eldon responded. And then he glanced down at the invitation. He blushed. "I shouldn't have looked at your mail but I just noticed it when I was organizing the stacks for this route." He glanced away. "I only saw that it was from South Carolina. That's all I read about it, I swear." He paused. "I'm sorry I looked and I'm sorry I brought it up a little while ago."

Beatrice shook her head. "Eldon, I am not upset that you notice postmarks on my mail."

"I could lose my job for telling you what I saw," he noted.

"You're not going to lose your job. I'm not telling anybody anything," Bea responded.

There was a pause. A car pulled down the street in front of Bea's house. They honked their horn as it was a neighbor who knew both Bea and Eldon. Eldon waved, but Bea just dropped her head again.

"I just came to tell you that I'm sorry that I yelled at you about Lily. I didn't mean to snap." He kept waiting for Beatrice to look at him but she did not. "I came back to apologize for that and to let you know I wasn't going postal or anything," he added.

"My daughter's getting married and I found out from the wedding invitation," she explained, not paying attention at all to his apology.

"Robin?" Eldon asked. He knew all of Beatrice's family. He grew up with the three children and was the same age as Beatrice's son. "That's odd," he said. And then he explained, "I never thought she was the marrying type."

"Well, neither did I," Beatrice said. "But I guess we are both wrong. I guess she's been the marrying type all along, she's just not the type who shares this information with her mother."

Eldon glanced around. He looked at his watch. He had a lot of mail to deliver but he knew he couldn't leave Beatrice as she was. He dropped his bag of mail by his side and sat down next to his old friend.

"Who is it?" he asked, referring to Robin's fiancé.

"Somebody by the name of Farrell Monk," she replied. "Sounds like a priest with rabies or some mental disorder, doesn't it?" she asked.

Eldon laughed and shook his head. "I wouldn't know about that," he replied.

"What kind of child doesn't tell her mother she's engaged? What kind of daughter lets her mother find out she's getting married from an invitation? An invitation that she sends to acquaintances and coworkers and people she doesn't even care about?" Bea wiped her nose on the sleeve of her blouse. "I feel like I don't even know her anymore. Or Jenny or Teddy. What happened to my relationships with my children?"

Eldon shrugged. He certainly didn't have the answers Beatrice was looking for. "Maybe she's afraid you won't like Farrell," he suggested. "Maybe she's embarrassed because he's short or has a lot of nose hairs or something."

Beatrice looked up at her mailman. "Nose hairs?" she asked. "Are you intending to be ridiculous or is this how you usually try and comfort your friends?"

He leaned over and bumped Beatrice with his shoulder. "I'm just saying maybe it isn't you as much as it is her." He rocked back to his seated position. "Robin was always a little, I don't know, different."

Beatrice studied Eldon. "What do you mean, different?" she asked.

He pulled a string from the edge of his jacket. "She was always real private about everything," he answered. "Sort of lived in a tight shell." He looked out across the street he had walked for most of his adult life. He was remembering the young girl he used to tease when they were teenagers. "It wasn't just you," he noted. "Robin never seemed to open up to anybody."

"How come you know so much about my daughter?" Bea asked, surprised to hear her mailman speaking about one of her children.

"We went out a few times," he confessed. "When she came home from college."

"You and Robin?" Bea asked.

"Yes. And why does that seem so hard to believe?" he responded, sounding hurt that Beatrice would act so shocked that he had dated Robin. "What, you think I'm good enough for Lily Bitterman but not your daughter?"

She leaned into him that time, bumping him so hard he almost fell. "I would have loved it if you and Robin had become a serious couple. Then she would have stayed close to home and I could have grandbabies that you could deliver when you brought my mail."

Eldon laughed. "You know that Robin was never going to stay in Hope Springs," he said. "That's part of the reason we didn't last. Well, that and I suppose I'm not that great of a catch." He dropped his head. "We can ask Lily about that."

"Eldon Macintyre, the only reason Lily Bitterman dropped you is because you wouldn't marry her. A woman has a ticking clock on these matters, you know."

There was a hesitation from Eldon before he answered.

"I asked Lily to marry me," he confessed.

The news seemed to shock Beatrice. She turned to look closely at her young friend.

"About once a year for fifteen years," he added. "She said no every time."

"Well, my Lord," Bea responded. She paused to think about what she had just heard. "Well, good riddance to her," she noted. "I never thought she had much sense anyway," she added. "And what else don't I know about my children?"

Eldon turned to look at Beatrice. "Probably a lot," he replied. "And if you didn't like Lily, why were you always trying to get us married?" he asked.

Beatrice shrugged. "I don't know. I just like the thought of people together," she replied. "It's not right to live your life alone. Everybody needs a mate," she added. "It's just the way we're meant to be."

The two of them watched as the Hurleys, a couple from up the street, walked hand in hand on the sidewalk in front of them. They all waved at each other.

"Nice day," Mr. Hurley called out.

"Lovely," Beatrice responded.

Eldon and Beatrice waited, watching the two as they crossed to the other side of the street.

"Good Lord," Beatrice whispered. "And to think he was almost dead eighteen years ago after his first wife died. Then he married Wanda and now he's about to pass the one hundred mark. I guess it just goes to show I'm right."

Eldon waited. "About what?" he finally asked.

"We all live longer and better with good love," she replied.

"I guess," Eldon responded, and he paused a moment. He turned to face Beatrice. "Then you should be glad for Robin," he said. "I know your feelings are hurt and you'll need to talk to her about her decision and why she didn't tell you in a more intimate way, but just be glad she's found somebody she loves because that's really a hard thing to do in this day and time."

Beatrice blew out a breath. She turned to Eldon and punched him in the side with her elbow. "Oh, what do you know? You're just the mailman."

They both laughed.

"No, I figure you're about right, Mr. Macintyre. And I'm going to try and listen to your advice."

"What?" Eldon asked, surprised to hear Beatrice put aside her hurt so quickly.

"I've worried about Robin all her life, that she'd be old and alone and miserable." She quickly turned to Eldon. "Not that I think you're going to be alone and miserable," she explained.

"It's all right, I understand," Eldon responded. "Finish what you were saying."

"If she's found her soul mate and he makes her happy, I'll be happy for the both of them. She must have her reasons for keeping things private and I'll respect that."

Eldon looked at Beatrice with a fair amount of suspicion. "You really mean that? You're going to let this go?" he asked.

"True dat," Bea replied.

Eldon seemed surprised by Bea's response, something he heard regularly on his favorite television show, *The Wire*. "I didn't know you watched HBO," he said.

"Oh no, I don't get HBO," she lied. "You would certainly know if I did because you'd see the bill," she added, sounding very guilty.

"Mrs. Witherspoon, I don't look at all of your mail," he replied, thinking that she was referring to how their conversation began and how he had noticed the wedding invitation from Robin. "You're not going to hold this one time that I did against me, are you?" he asked.

She patted Eldon on the leg and stood up, grateful that he hadn't seemed to catch on that she was not receiving the bills she should. "You're a good mailman, Eldon," she said. "And a good friend, and I would say nothing more or less than that to anyone who asked," she added.

Eldon stood up and grabbed his mailbag, tossing

it on his shoulder, relieved to hear that his customer wasn’t upset about what had happened. “I enjoyed our talk, Mrs. Witherspoon,” he said as he turned to walk down the steps. “Everything is going to be fine,” he added. “You just wait and scc.”

“True dat,” she said again, softly.

And Eldon smiled, headed down the steps, opened the gate, and went back to work.

Water Chestnut-Bacon Wraps

2 5-ounce cans water chestnuts
½ cup soy sauce
sugar
slices of bacon, cut thin

Soak water chestnuts in soy sauce for 1 hour or overnight. Roll chestnuts in sugar. Wrap them in slices of bacon and secure with toothpicks. Bake at 325 degrees for 25 to 30 minutes. Drain. Keep warm until serving.

—Reverend Tom Joles

Chapter Nine

Beatrice slid the invitation into her purse and got the keys to her car. She ran out of the house, slamming the door behind her, and wasn't thinking while she cranked the engine, put it in gear, and backed out of the driveway. She was headed in the direction of Hope Springs Church, down past the center of town, and out on Route 16. She drove as if she was of clear mind, but the truth was that she wasn't thinking about exactly where she intended to go.

She turned right onto the street behind the parsonage and into the little subdivision where several of the church members lived before she realized that she was driving straight toward Margaret's old house. When she understood what she was doing, she came to a complete stop in the middle of the road. Fortunately, there were no other cars around and she did a U-turn before she made it all the way to the familiar driveway.

She stopped at the stop sign, thinking about what she had done, thinking about how many times she had made that trip, gone to that house, driven down that driveway, and found her friend waiting for her at the front door. She had not been on that street in several months, and she was at least relieved that she hadn't gotten all the way to the house before she realized what she had done. She had heard that the land and the house had been sold not long after Margaret died, and she had never driven by it again.

Beatrice hit the gas and drove straight back to the church. She turned off the engine once she had pulled into the parking lot. She sat in the car, beating her fists against the steering wheel, crying, and shouting to no one.

"Damn you, Margaret Peele. Damn you, damn you, damn you!" she screamed. "What am I supposed to do without you? What on earth am I supposed to do? You were the one who taught me how to be a good mother. You were the one who told me what to do with my girls. You taught me everything, and now I need you to teach me again and you're gone. Dead and gone!"

Beatrice dropped her head against the steering wheel and cried, and then she reached into her purse and took out the wedding invitation and began to rip it apart. She threw the pieces on the floorboard.

"Have your nice wedding in Mexico! Have your nice life with Farrell Monk! I hope I never have to see you again!" Beatrice yelled at the top of her lungs.

She thought about Robin, how betrayed she felt by her daughter. She was broken by the betrayal and embarrassed that her own child wouldn't want her to be a part of this experience. She balled her fists and beat the steering wheel again, and then she dropped her head and cried even more.

She wasn't sure how long she had been like that when she felt someone standing beside her car door. The person was peering in at her through the window. She lifted her head and realized it was the pastor of Hope Springs, Reverend Tom Joles.

He nodded at her when she looked up at him. "You okay, Beatrice?" he asked, leaning down toward her.

Beatrice didn't know this pastor very well. Like the other women in the cookbook committee, she missed Charlotte. Reverend Joles was nice enough, handled his business well enough, but it was just never the same at church once Charlotte moved away. Beatrice and Dick remained active in the congregation, but her heart had not been in her work there in a long time.

Beatrice turned on the engine for power and rolled down the window. She wiped her face on the sleeve of her coat. "No, Pastor, I'm definitely not okay. I'm having a nervous breakdown but I'd prefer to be alone, if you don't mind." She turned away and stared straight ahead, toward the cemetery. She hoped that he wouldn't push her to give more information or ask to call Dick or Jessie or Louise. She wanted to be left alone, just as she had asked.

The preacher stood up, nodding his head, biting the inside of his lip, like he was thinking. "All right then," he said, tapping the window with his finger, and turned slowly to walk back to the church office.

Beatrice watched him in her rearview mirror, surprised that he had abided by her wishes and was not going to demand she talk to him. She was shocked that he was giving her exactly what she had asked. She blew out a long breath and followed him in the mirror.

He didn't go inside the church, but rather he sat down on a bench near the back of the building, near the office door. The children from the preschool had just come out in the adjacent playground and he was sitting there, apparently enjoying their play.

Beatrice looked back at her own reflection in the mirror. She was a mess. Her makeup had been wiped away; the mascara she had put on earlier was smeared all the way down her cheeks. Her eyes were puffy and red.

"No wonder he didn't put up a fight about leaving me alone," she said to herself, dabbing at her face with a tissue. She touched up the sides of her hair and looked back in the direction of the church and at her pastor sitting on the bench. She took in a deep breath, turned the engine off, and unbuckled her seat belt. She got out of the car and headed in his direction.

She stood next to him for a few seconds before speaking. She watched the children as they squealed in delight, running from one toy to another. A couple of little girls were swinging on the swing set, a few were sliding down the slide, and one little boy was sitting in the sandbox, playing with trucks. A light winter breeze blew, and Beatrice pulled her jacket together and zipped it. It was sunny but still cold. The landscape around them was barren, deep in the middle of February and winter.

"I do love sitting out here and watching them play," the pastor announced without turning around to Beatrice. "Somehow, it doesn't matter what my day is like, if I just make the time to sit out here and watch them, see how they get along, how they laugh and jump and run, how they are so delighted with themselves and life, well, it just somehow settles me." He turned around to his parishioner, still standing behind him. He paused for a second. "You want to join me?" he finally asked.

Beatrice smiled a weak smile and walked around to take a seat beside the older gentleman.

Reverend Joles had been at Hope Springs Community Church for about three years, but Beatrice had never spent more than a few minutes with him. She brought him prune cakes, as she did for every pastor, and did anything he asked her to do. She made calls to the homebound members, took communion to the sick, hosted fellowship hour after worship or during special events.

She was the recording secretary for the Women's Fellowship and she never missed a Sunday, but in all the time that he had been there, Beatrice never took the time to get to know Reverend Joles or his wife.

She realized as she sat there beside him that she really didn't know anything about him. So unlike herself, Beatrice had not pestered him for personal information or details about his life before coming to Hope Springs. She hadn't invited the couple over to the house for a meal. She hadn't dropped by the office to get to know him better. She hadn't gone to the parsonage to drop off leftovers or to see how he and his wife had decorated the place. Once Charlotte left and Margaret got sick, Bea simply lost interest in new folks, even the pastor of her beloved church.

"Is that Nadine's little boy?" she asked, referring to the child in the sandbox.

"Jackson," the preacher answered. "He's four this year," he added. "And that's Laura and Billie, and the little one on the slide is Austin." He pointed to the little boy just getting ready to slide down. "He's Edie and Pete's grandson," he said.

Beatrice glanced over at the pastor. She didn't know that he had taken such a personal interest in the children at the day care center. Somehow, hearing that he knew all the children's names surprised her.

She looked back at the children and shook her

head slowly. "Four years old," she noted, referring to the little boy about whom she had first asked. "It's hard to believe Nadine has been married that long and has another baby." She thought for a second. "It's hard to believe that it's been almost ten years since little Brittany died." She felt the tears welling up in her eyes. She was an emotional mess at this point. Any memory was enough to set her up for a weeping jag.

There was a pause.

"I remember hearing about that death," Reverend Joles responded. "Your pastor did a wonderful job caring for this community after that tragedy." He pulled out his handkerchief and handed it to Beatrice, without ever looking at her. "There can't be anything harder for a family or a community than the death of a child."

"It broke us," Bea said, recalling the death, the funeral, and the aftermath. She remembered Nadine and her suicide attempt, Charlotte's coping skills of working long hours at the church, Jessie's poignant prayers that she would stand in the congregation and pray every Sunday morning, and she remembered Margaret and her way of gathering everyone to her and holding them, the way she gave so much comfort with just her presence.

Beatrice thought of Margaret and she started crying again. She dropped her head in her hands, and the pastor waited a minute and then placed his hand on her shoulder.

"You missing Margaret?" he asked, surprising Beatrice that he knew what was wrong.

She looked up at him and nodded her head. "She was my best friend," Beatrice explained. "She was loyal and smart and she could tell me what to do right now," she added.

There was a pause before the pastor spoke.

"Margaret Peele was as fine a person as I have ever known," Reverend Joles noted.

"She was that," Beatrice added. She wiped her eyes.

There was another pause in the conversation.

"You know, in the same way that after Nadine's little girl died there was a pall cast over this church, I sort of feel as if a sorrow has settled on this community since Margaret passed. I just get the feeling we're all kind of stuck in some kind of an old grief." He pulled his hand away, and Beatrice leaned back against the bench.

Beatrice didn't respond right away. She thought about what the pastor was saying. She thought it seemed quite accurate about the folks at Hope Springs.

"I suppose you're right," she agreed. "Margaret was the spiritual center of this church. Without her, I just feel like we've lost our foundation." She blew her nose on the handkerchief and then realized how what she had said might have offended the spiritual leader of Hope Springs Church. She tried to correct herself. "I don't mean you don't bring us a lot in your leadership, Pastor," she said. "I just, I . . ." Beatrice struggled for the words.

"You don't need to worry about my feelings," Reverend Joles interrupted. "I know what you mean." He dropped his hands on his lap. "And you're right, she was the foundation for this church. She was like the flight attendant on a plane."

Beatrice glanced over at the minister. "I don't follow you," she said, looking confused. "Margaret hated to fly."

Reverend Joles smiled. "I don't mean literally, Bea," he responded.

Beatrice nodded.

"Have you ever flown?" he asked her.

"Of course," Beatrice replied.

"Have you ever been on a flight that was maybe bumpy or turbulent?"

Beatrice considered the question. She nodded.

"Did you notice how when that happens, everybody looks at the flight attendant?"

Beatrice thought about the time she flew with Dick to Florida and there was a thunderstorm. She recalled how the plane rocked and dipped and how she had been scared to death. She realized that Reverend Joles was right. She had looked at the flight attendant who was working in the section of the airplane where Beatrice was sitting. The woman had been serving drinks at the time, and she never missed a beat. She kept taking orders and pouring soda and juice and water and never cast a look of fear or worry. She never glanced out the window or turned to look at another flight attendant. She just went along with business as usual. And it had calmed Beatrice, and as she remembered the flight she understood what the pastor was trying to explain.

"Everybody looks at the flight attendant to see how she's acting," he continued. "They watch her to see if she is upset or nervous, and if she isn't, everybody feels comforted, hopeful. They know that if she's not upset, everything is going to be okay."

Beatrice nodded, completely understanding. "Margaret was our point of reference for how we should be," she said. "Everybody looked at her, looked to her, to know whether we should be upset or concerned."

"Or not," Reverend Joles added.

"Or not," Beatrice repeated. She started to cry again. "And now we don't have a flight attendant and I feel like my plane is falling from the sky." She shook her head. "And I don't know where to look for comfort or help or instruction."

The pastor didn't respond for a while. He just sat while Beatrice cried. Finally, he leaned forward, glanced over at Beatrice, and spoke. "Beatrice, I will never be Margaret and I can't be Reverend Stewart, but I would like to be your friend, if you'd let me. I know it's been hard to accept me here and I've respected that difficulty for all the time I've been at Hope Springs." He cleared his throat. "But I'm kind of lonesome too," he added. "It would mean a lot to me for you and the others just to let me in, a little." He cleared his throat again, and Beatrice looked. "I miss her too," he said. "I miss Margaret Peele too."

The two sat there for a few minutes without speaking until a couple of the children came over to the fence that surrounded the playground and stared at the two grown-ups sitting on the bench near them.

One of them, a little girl about five years old, called out, "Pastor Tom, are you and that lady all right?"

He smiled at the little girl. "Libby, I think we're both going to be okay," he replied. "And you are very sweet to come over and check on us," he added.

The little girl grinned. "Well, Pastor Tom, you said that you were my friend, and making sure you're okay is what friends do," she said, sounding very much as if she thought the minister ought to know that already. Then she shrugged and took the hand of the little girl standing beside her, and they turned and ran back to the swing set.

Beatrice turned to look at the pastor. "Margaret would want me to ask you for help," she said. "She probably was the one who sent you to me today," she added.

Reverend Joles smiled and took Beatrice by the hand. "And what kind of help are you needing, my friend?" he asked.

"Well, Pastor," she confessed. "It's kind of a long story but it starts with a wedding in Mexico."

"That sounds like a movie I just watched last night," he remarked. "Do you get HBO?" he asked.

"I am planning to pay for those channels!" she yelled, and the pastor looked at her in confusion.

"Okay," he responded.

All the children and teachers on the playground turned and looked in their direction.

"I'm sorry," she apologized to the reverend, and then spoke loudly enough for the others to hear. "I'm sorry." She waved at them with the handkerchief, and they returned to their play. "I'm still just a little upset," she said to Reverend Joles, realizing she still had his handkerchief. She handed it back to him.

He glanced down at the dirty handkerchief. "Just keep that, Beatrice."

She nodded and placed it back on her lap.

"So, your story starts with a wedding in Mexico." He repeated what she had said earlier.

The two of them stopped talking and watched as the teacher called for the children to assemble into a line and follow her into the building. The children laughed and shouted as they walked inside. In the back of the line, Libby, just before heading through the door, turned and waved. And the two adults, smiling at the little girl as she left the playground, waved together, looking a lot like old friends.

Chile con Queso

4 tablespoons butter
1 large onion, finely chopped
2 cloves garlic, minced
2 tablespoons all-purpose flour
1 cup light cream
2 10-ounce cans chopped tomatoes
2 8-ounce packages Montercy Jack cheese, shredded
1 4-ounce can hot chopped green chiles

Melt butter in a large skillet and sauté onion and garlic. Sprinkle flour while stirring. Add cream and tomatoes to ingredients in skillet. Bring to a slight boil and simmer 2 minutes, stirring. Add the cheese a half cup at a time, keeping the heat turned down. Add chiles.

—Janice B.

Chapter Ten

Carla was awake, dressed, and sitting at the dining room table when Charlotte walked in the back door for work. Janice, Iris, Denise, Martha, and her two small children, both girls, were all sitting with her, eating breakfast. The four other adult residents and the two children had plans for the day, and Charlotte had been hoping that she would have some time alone with Carla to talk about the recent events that had brought her into St. Mary's.

"Well, don't all of you look chipper and ready to face the morning?" Charlotte commented as she closed the door behind her. Her arms were full of shopping bags because she had stopped by the Goodwill Center to find Carla some things to wear. She knew that most of the clothes at St. Mary's would be too large for a woman as petite as she was.

The manager at the donation center usually allowed Charlotte to shop before they opened the store. The two women became friends when the manager, a victim of domestic abuse, had stayed a couple of weeks at St. Mary's after Charlotte first arrived in Gallup. Charlotte had helped the woman land the managerial position at Goodwill, and in return she liked being able to do anything she could for the residents of St. Mary's. She donated most of the clothes to the shelter. She also gave them furniture and books and anything else the women needed.

"You already been shopping?" Denise asked. She walked over to help Charlotte carry some of the bags. "You find anything in a twelve?" She opened one of the bags and peered inside.

"Here," Charlotte said, handing her another bag. "This one is yours."

Denise smiled and yanked the bag from Charlotte. She put the other bags she was holding on the floor. "Did you get a skirt?" she asked, and before Charlotte could answer she pulled out a long dark blue skirt. "You are so fabulous, Sister Charlotte!" she exclaimed. And she ran out of the room to try it on.

"Wait!" Charlotte yelled. "You forgot the blazer."

Denise flew back into the room and grabbed the bag from Charlotte, who was still standing in the doorway holding it. "It's a suit!" she yelled in delight. "I have a suit!" And she turned and ran down the hall.

"She's wanted a nice suit for three months," Martha explained to Carla, who appeared surprised at what had just happened. "She's been studying to be a court reporter and she was told that she has to have a dark suit to get the job."

Carla nodded and then quickly looked away

from the other woman. Charlotte could see that there hadn't been a lot of conversation or eye contact before she had arrived. She took the bags and dropped them off in her office. She would show her findings to Carla when everyone left.

Charlotte walked back into the dining room and noticed everyone as they watched Carla trying unsuccessfully to eat her first spoonful of cereal. With the injuries she had suffered, she couldn't open her mouth wide enough for the spoon, and once she realized that, she just put the spoon back in the bowl. The other women glanced away, ashamed they had been staring. There was an awkward silence at the table.

"Why don't I fix you a milk shake?" Charlotte asked.

Just as she asked the question, Darlene walked into the room behind her. "I will fix the milk shake," she announced. "Because I am the queen of shake," she added.

The little girls were watching and they both clapped their hands. "I want one too!" the younger one cried.

"You don't need no milk shake," Martha said, pushing the bowl of cereal closer to her daughter. "You can eat your cereal." And the little girl pouted but took up her spoon and continued eating.

Darlene went into the kitchen and over to the freezer, got the ice cream, opened the refrigerator, pulled out the milk and some blueberries, and then went over to the counter, cut half of a banana, and then slid the blender toward her. She mixed everything together, grabbed a tall glass from the cabinet, and poured the contents from the blender into the glass. She found a straw and then walked into the dining room and put the concoction in front of Carla. "I had my mouth wired together for six weeks after my jaw was broken. I can make any kind of milk shake you want." She smiled and walked back into the kitchen and poured herself a cup of coffee.

"Thank you," Carla mumbled.

The women all nodded their approval.

"So, who needs a ride this morning?" Charlotte asked, smiling. The tenderness she observed among the women at the shelter always touched her deeply. She knew the kindness, the easy way they had with one another, the knowing way they spoke to one another, was the very best medicine the women would ever receive. She walked around with the coffeepot and began refilling the women's cups.

"It's all being handled," Janice announced, waving away any more coffee and clearing away her dishes to take them into the kitchen to put into the dishwasher. "I'm taking Martha and Denise and the girls. Darlene is driving Iris to her doctor's appointment. We're all in good shape, Sister."

She finished her cleaning and walked over to Charlotte, who had placed the coffeepot back in the maker and was standing in the doorway. Janice pinched her on the cheek. "And so now you can call your cute police officer we all saw you drooling over last night and tell him the coast is clear for a private visit." She winked. "I'm sure Carla here won't mind staying in her room for a couple of hours."

Charlotte blushed and turned to Carla, who was sipping her milk shake and had been watching, but then had quickly looked away from the executive director. Charlotte wasn't sure what Carla knew about the relationship Charlotte had with her ex-husband, but she was sure that the other women didn't realize that Carla had once been married to the police officer they had seen at the shelter the previous night.

"Oooh," Martha started in then. *"Sister Charlotte has a boyfriend,"* she sang. Her little girls giggled and joined their mother in the chorus, *"Sister Charlotte has a boyfriend!"*

Charlotte felt her face start to flush. "I think it's time for you all to get going," she said loudly, but she was still unable to stop the women from teasing.

"Give us the scoop and we'll leave you alone," Martha said, grinning.

"There is no scoop," Charlotte answered, trying to hurry the women away from the table and out of the dining room, trying to put a halt to the awkward conversation. "We are making a bad impression on our newest resident." She pleaded for them to stop.

"So, how did you meet Officer Tall, Dark, and Handsome?" Darlene wanted to know.

"How many times have you gone out?" Martha chimed in.

"Have you kissed him?" Hannah asked, laughing. She was the older of Martha's two girls. Josie was six and Hannah was eight. The two girls became unglued with that question and fell out of their chairs laughing.

At that moment Denise walked into the room to model her new suit. "What did I miss?" she asked, suddenly aware that something important had been going on while she was not in the kitchen.

"Nothing, Denise, and you look wonderful. It fits you perfectly and you will make a fabulous court reporter." Charlotte clapped her hands together like a teacher. "Now, Hannah and Josie, you both need to get ready for school," she reported loudly, and quickly walked over to the two girls and helped them to the floor. "Let's go get your teeth brushed while your mommy cleans up the dishes." She shot a look over to Martha, and before any of the women could say anything else, she ushered the girls out of the room.

"I didn't know Sister Charlotte was kissing a man," Iris, the oldest of the residents, said quietly. And the women burst out laughing so that

Charlotte could hear them even though she was down the hall.

Disappointed that there was going to be no more gossip, the women finished their breakfasts and their coffee and quickly cleaned up the dining room and kitchen, and within a few minutes were all dressed and out the door. All the previously made arrangements among the residents left Charlotte alone with Carla, who was still sitting at the table drinking her milk shake. Once the women were out of the house, however, Charlotte was embarrassed about the breakfast conversation and how the women had teased her about Donovan in front of his ex-wife. With all that information about Donovan and Charlotte being unloaded in front of Carla, Charlotte wasn't sure how to start a dialogue with St. Mary's newest resident. She wiped down the counter while Carla moved into the kitchen and sat at the small kitchen table.

"Was Darlene's milk shake okay?" Charlotte finally broke the ice.

"It's good," Carla responded.

Charlotte placed the dishrag over the faucet and poured herself a cup of coffee. She walked over to the table and sat down across from Carla.

"It's quiet when they all leave, isn't it?" Charlotte asked.

Carla didn't respond. She took a sip of her drink.

"Laurie told me that she gave you something for the pain. Did it help last night?" Charlotte had talked to the nurse after she had completed the examination. She had reported exactly what Carla had already suspected. More than likely, there were a couple of broken ribs. Everything else was probably just bruised or sprained. She suggested taking a few X-rays, just to make sure, but Carla had refused any further medical attention, and so Laurie had treated her with bandages, ice packs, a heating pad, and Percocet.

Carla nodded gently. It was easy to see that the slightest movement was still very painful.

The two women sat at the table. Neither of them appeared to be very comfortable in the situation.

"Donnie told me that he had been out with you," Carla said. "When he was bringing me here, he told me how you had met."

Charlotte nodded. "I don't know what to say, Carla, I'm sorry."

Carla looked up at Charlotte. "What do you have to be sorry about?" she asked.

Charlotte shrugged. "I don't know. I'm sorry that you had to be here when the girls were giving me a hard time. I'm sorry that it feels so awkward this morning."

Carla glanced back down at the table. She stuck the straw in her mouth and took another sip of her drink. "Donnie is a good guy. He deserves to have love," she said, surprising Charlotte.

Charlotte nodded. She took a sip of her coffee. "You want to talk about it?" she asked. This was usually the way she began a conversation with a new client at St. Mary's, and she was comfortable with that beginning. This one seemed a little different, but, she reminded herself, she had never been dating the ex-husband of one of her clients before.

"You mean about me and Donnie or me and Bo?" Carla asked.

Charlotte thought the response was fair. She would have asked the same thing. "Is Bo your husband's name?" Charlotte responded. She hadn't gotten very much personal information about the man who beat her from Donovan or from Carla the night before.

Carla nodded slowly. "We've been married six years," she added, and Charlotte recalled Donovan telling her that much. "It's never been this bad," she said. "He was really mad last night."

Charlotte waited for more of the story. She never liked to push the women to tell more than they were comfortable telling, especially just after arriving at the shelter. Charlotte understood that by the time most of these women had gotten to St. Mary's they had been forced to tell a lot of information to a lot of people, including the perpetrator, who often beat the victim because he thought she was keeping something from him.

"He got mad because he heard I had called Donnie last week," she confessed. "Bo hates

Donnie even though I don't think they've ever even met," she added.

Charlotte took another sip of coffee.

"Bo hates all police officers, and when we first met and he found out I had been married to one, he's hated them even more."

"Why did you call Donnie last week?" Charlotte asked, and then wished she hadn't. It sounded more like the question from a jealous girlfriend than from a concerned professional.

Carla didn't seem to mind the question or to think much about it. "I was scared," she said. "Bo was getting more and more violent, and I thought I needed to talk to Donnie to find out where I could go."

Charlotte nodded. She wondered what day of the previous week Donovan had talked to his ex-wife, wondered if it had coincided with the night they had gone out. She tried to shake those thoughts from her mind.

"How did Bo find out?" Charlotte asked.

Carla shook her head. She placed her bandaged arm on the table and then, grimacing, put it back in her lap. "I don't know. I don't know how he finds out anything. He has spies, he tells me." Having finished her milk shake, she sat back in her chair. She looked up at Charlotte. "Do you think they got him last night?" she asked, sounding a bit nervous.

Charlotte answered confidently, "Donovan called this morning. Your husband was arrested and charged. He's in jail. They booked him after they woke him up," she added, alluding to the fact that he was passed out when they got to their residence.

Carla smiled slightly, understanding what she meant. "I hit him with a skillet," she confessed.

Charlotte drank the last of her coffee. "And pretty good, I heard," she responded.

The two women waited for a minute before continuing their conversation.

"Will he come after me here?" Carla asked.

Charlotte waited before answering. She knew this was the fear of every woman who stayed at St. Mary's. She knew the risks the battered women took in leaving their abusive relationships. She knew the efforts she and Maria and Laurie and all the other volunteers, all of the board members, took to keep the location of St. Mary's private. She spoke to the workers and residents more about the need for privacy and keeping the location of the shelter secret than about anything else.

She knew the fear she felt when some of the women left and went back to their abusive partners and how she was always worried that they would tell the violent men the address of the shelter. Charlotte loved her work, was passionate in dealing with the issue of domestic violence, would do anything for any of those women she housed; but Charlotte was also always a little afraid herself that one of these men, who could beat and kill their wives and girlfriends and family members, would come to St. Mary's and do violence to her or to those entrusted to her care.

"He'll never find us," Charlotte finally answered, sounding as confident as she could. "I've been here a long time, and none of the men have ever come here," she added, glad to remind herself of these statistics. "He'll be in jail awhile, and when he gets out, we'll have found you a new place to live."

Carla seemed comforted by this news.

"Do you have family or anybody we could call?" Charlotte asked, going back to her standard questions asked during an intake of a new resident.

"Donnie called my sister in Farmington," she replied. "I guess my mother knows too."

Charlotte got up from the table, taking her mug and Carla's glass. She washed and dried them both and put them in the cabinet. "I brought you some clothes. I figured you were a size four petite. Is that about right?" she asked.

Carla smiled and nodded. "You're pretty good at this," she said.

"We're going to take good care of you, Carla," Charlotte promised.

"Donnie hasn't dated anybody seriously since me," Carla said.

Charlotte nodded, helping Carla up from the table. She was surprised to hear Carla mention this.

"I hope you'll give him a chance even though it's . . ." She hesitated. ". . . complicated," she finished.

Charlotte smiled and walked with Carla down the hall and toward her office to get the bag of clothes. She didn't respond to the remark made by the newest resident at St. Mary's. She simply wasn't sure what to say.

Spinach Surprise

1 package frozen chopped spinach
4 slices bacon
¼ stick margarine
1 pound sharp cheddar cheese, shredded
1 small onion, minced
½ cup flour
½ cup whole milk
½ teaspoon baking powder
2 eggs, beaten
½ teaspoon salt
pepper to taste

After cooking and draining the spinach, cook bacon until crisp, crumble it, and set the bacon aside. Melt the margarine in a 9-inch pan. Mix all the ingredients, except the bacon crumbles, and pour into pan. Sprinkle the bacon over the top. Bake at 350 degrees for 30 minutes and let cool before serving.

—From Roxie Cannon's recipes

Chapter Eleven

Louise could not make up her mind about getting married, and she was angry with herself that she couldn't just tell George no. He had called her every day in the last week from Baltimore, trying not to sound desperate and plead, but certainly working to persuade Louise to give him an answer. His condition was worsening more quickly than originally expected. He was eager to start his new life, this new life that would soon be death. He needed her to marry him, and he needed her to do it soon.

Louise heard the phone ring and she didn't move from the swing on her back deck. She was sure that it was George since he had promised last week to call again, giving her a few more days to decide. She knew he had waited as long as he could and then dialed her number again. Four times the phone signaled a call, and finally the voice mail picked up. She would check it later even though she was sure she knew who it was.

It was a cool April day and Louise was enjoying being outside. She closed her eyes and pushed herself back and forth with her feet. She loved her old porch swing. She loved the back deck and the way the sun danced between branches of trees and the way breezes stirred while she rested there. Even when she had been advised to cut some of the trees closest to her house, she had kept all of them in the backyard. She was often nervous during ice storms when the trunks would splinter and the limbs break, but then spring and summer would soon take the place of winter and she would laugh at her worries and enjoy the ample shade, knowing that even on the hottest days it would be cool out there. She loved her backyard.

It had been Roxie's favorite spot on the property as well. Even when she was agitated, the Alzheimer's yanking her further and further away from reality, shifting her thoughts from long ago to even longer ago, Louise could bring Roxie outside, ease her into the swing, push her just a little, and the agitation would lessen. Roxie would smile and cluck her tongue against the roof of her mouth, mimicking the sound of the woodpecker they could hear working on one of the hardwood trees at the edge of the backyard. The light breeze would blow through her hair and she would lay her head back and cluck.

Louise smiled, wrapping the light blanket around herself, recalling those last months she spent with Roxie. They were splendid and horrible, both at the same time. It was a constant battle, trying to convince Roxie who she was, trying to convince Roxie that she wasn't in a stranger's house, that she wouldn't be harmed. Every day was a struggle with Roxie's sense of loss, her unexplainable grief in having everything taken from her, her capability to reason, her family, the ability to recognize people she was told she should know. And yet even in the struggles, the day-to-day battles, the cajoling and the arguing and the convincing, there had been the most amazing moments of tenderness, of sweet, intimate communion for Louise and Roxie. There had been these quick but satisfying moments when Roxie would look right into Louise's eyes and tell her thank you or that she loved her, and even though they were as fast as lightning, gone in a blink of an eye, they were there, and those were the moments that made for most of Louise's memories.

When Roxie died, Louise was glad her friend didn't have to suffer any longer, but if it had been up to her and she was allowed to be completely selfish about things, she would have kept Roxie alive for as long as she could, just to have one more of those clear and beautiful moments.

"So, what do you think of this arrangement, Miss Roxie Ann?" Louise asked the question out loud, imagining her friend sitting next to her in the swing.

"Your husband asking me to marry him, it's ridiculous, isn't it? And I am crazy for even considering such a thing, right?" She draped her arm across the back of the swing the way she used to do when Roxie was beside her. Back and forth she pushed the swing, thinking of her best friend and all the days they had together.

Louise drifted back in her memories and thought about Roxie when she was young, how simply she saw the world, how matter-of-fact she could be. Louise let the morning breeze move her back and forward in the swing and suddenly remembered a time when the two women lived together in a boardinghouse while they worked at the mill, a time when Louise asked her friend for advice regarding her relationship with her mother.

Louise had never been close to her family and she was particularly distant from her mother, a harsh woman who openly displayed her disapproval of Louise and her sisters. All her childhood, Louise had felt as if she had never been quite good enough for her mother, never been able to measure up to her mother's standards. Her mother had often told her daughter that because she was so stupid and ugly, she would never amount to anything more than a dirt farmer's wife. Louise's mother had refused to buy her children new clothes or spend any money on them at all, so Louise and her sisters learned at a very early age how to sew their own dresses and blouses, and they shared what they had with one another and accepted hand-me-downs from cousins and friends. By the time Louise was a teenager, out of school, and had moved out of town to work on her own, she and her mother barely spoke.

One day she received a letter from her mother asking Louise to send home more money. Louise already sent a large portion of what she made to her parents, leaving her with very little to make ends meet. She had left home to get away from her mother and to join her sisters at the mill, and even though she had no tenderness toward her parents, she still felt a responsibility to help support them, to send them money.

Louise knew things on the farm were difficult; her father had suffered a back injury a year before she left and was not able to do the work of planting and harvesting, and her mother had never been one to work outside. She spoke in the same harsh way to her husband as she did to her children, always belittling him, always reminding him how she hated him for being a farmer, and she refused to help him in any way. In the earlier years, Louise and her siblings had been the ones to milk the cow or feed the hogs, hoe the rows of beans and cucumbers, and drive the tractor through the fields. The children had managed all the outdoor chores, including planting and growing the gardens and taking care of the livestock. Louise's mother would cook meals and clean the house, but she would never venture outside beyond a small flower garden she kept near the back door to the kitchen.

When her father was injured and most of the children were gone, the farmland became barren, and the yard and the vegetable gardens were unattended to and unproductive. Louise, like her sisters, left the farm and the unhappy surroundings, but they still supported their parents by sending money from their paychecks. All of them hated to leave their father, worried about him, but in the end only one brother, the oldest son, could stand to live close by. He did as much as he could, growing tobacco and cotton, but he too depended on his sisters' assistance. None of them discussed how much each one of them was sending, and Louise, unaware at the time that she was sending more than any of the others, was seeking advice from her friend after receiving the letter from home demanding more money.

"Did Maxine or Deborah get a letter like that?" Roxie had asked when she heard about the correspondence. She was referring to Louise's sisters.

"I don't know," Louise answered.

"Don't you think you ought to ask them?"

Louise and Roxie had been sitting on the front porch of the boardinghouse. It was a Saturday, and neither of them had to work. They were planning to take a drive out to a lake. George and a few other boys were going with them.

"Why would it matter whether or not they got the same letter as I did?" Louise responded. "She's still asking me for money."

"Louise, how much do you send your mother?" Roxie was leaning against the porch railing. Over the years that they had been working and living together, she had made a few critical comments about Louise's constant contributions to her parents, but she had never confronted her friend and she had never asked such a personal question.

"I send her half," Louise replied.

"Every month?"

Louise nodded.

"Do you save anything?" Roxie asked, surprised to hear the answer.

Louise shook her head. "After rent and groceries and gas, there isn't really anything left to save."

"And now she's asking for more?"

Louise recalled how Roxie had bent close to her at that point, knelt down in front of her, in fact, putting her hands on Louise's knees. She recalled the words Roxie had said that endeared her friend to her even more.

"Louise, you are a good person. You are the best friend I have ever had and you are a good sister and a good daughter. But understand that you will never hear these words from your mother. She does not see you for who you are and she probably never will. Sending your father a little money every month is a kind and generous thing to do. It is honorable, and I think you should keep doing that. But you cannot buy what you want from your mother, and you do not have to try and repay her for being your parent." She had stood up at that point and leaned over Louise.

"You and your sisters need to talk and decide

upon the amount you are going to send your parents, and then you need to save some money for yourself. And you need to get out from under your mother's cloud. It is time to be your own woman and to take care of and love yourself."

And Louise had taken Roxie's advice. She and her sisters had talked, and that was when she discovered how much more she was sending home than her siblings. Together, they decided upon a set amount, and they contributed toward that amount and refused to send more. Her mother had written some terrible letters following that decision, but Louise, with the help of Roxie, had stuck to her guns, and she was finally able to save enough money to buy her own car, her own house, and even go to community college and take a few courses.

"So, what would you tell me now, dear one?" Louise asked again after remembering that cherished story about Roxie's advice.

She envisioned her friend sitting beside her on the swing, her mind clear, her thoughts rational. She imagined Roxie snuggled next to her, the two of them sharing the blanket, Louise with her arm wrapped around Roxie's shoulder, and she could almost hear her voice.

"You do not owe George anything," she thought she could hear Roxie say. "He treated you badly when we were friends, and I know it was hard for you when I got married."

Louise smiled. She closed her eyes, listening to the make-believe conversation she was having.

"You are a good friend, an honorable woman, and you deserve to be happy in whatever way you define that."

Roxie would have taken her hand then, slid her long fingers in between Louise's short, stumpy ones. And they would have sat like that for hours without needing to say another word between them. The shadows lengthened as the morning edged into the afternoon.

"Do you still love George?" Louise asked the ghost of her friend who she pretended was beside her, the woman she remembered as being completely honest and straightforward.

"Of course I still love George," Louise was sure that Roxie would answer. "But that doesn't mean you owe me more than you've already given me. It doesn't mean you have to do something that isn't yours to do."

"So, maybe I want to know how it feels to be married. Maybe I want to see my name on some legal document that connects me to another human being. Maybe it would make me feel closer to you."

Louise waited for some reply from her dead friend, waited for some smart but imagined response from Roxie, but there was nothing else she could hear or sense, no counsel or wisdom or instruction. Just a sweet sense of peace and acceptance, the light breeze blowing around her, and the knowledge that she was already and completely loved by the one who had mattered most.

Louise blew out a long breath, opened her eyes, and made up her mind just as the phone started ringing.

James's Pigs in a Blanket

4 packages Pillsbury Crescent dinner rolls
16 8-inch sausages
2 eggs, lightly beaten
pinch salt
pepper to taste
hot sauce to taste

Unroll dinner roll dough without separating. Cut into 16 small rectangles. Cook sausages in skillet and cut each sausage into 4 equal parts. Roll each sausage in a rectangle of dough. Place on a lightly greased baking sheet. Combine eggs with spices and brush each sausage with egg mix. Bake at 375 degrees for about 10 to 15 minutes.

—James Jenkins

Chapter Twelve

Jessie was cleaning out the bedroom closet when the letter fell out from between two suitcases. She didn't notice it at first. She was standing on a stepladder, pulling down shoe boxes and cartons of wrapping paper and bows. Jessie enjoyed a good day of cleaning, and since the weatherman had called for a cold rain that particular day in April, it just seemed like a good time to sort and clean for a new season.

It wasn't until later, after she had finished arranging the luggage and the summer shoes and the plastic bags of extra sheets on the long shelf above the rack and had stepped down from the ladder, that she saw the faded envelope caught under the edge of the closet door. She bent down and picked it up.

It was addressed to James, postmarked in 1990-something, from Maryland, sent to his apartment in Washington, D.C., during the time he had left Jessie and was living out of state. The return address, written in the top left corner of the envelope, included just three initials, RWH, the letters, small and curled, offering no more information than just that. She held the letter in her hand, somehow feeling the weight of it, somehow knowing it was more than just a bill or random statement about investments or monies needed, that it was more than just a note giving information about a family gathering or news from home. Somehow, just the way his name was written, so matched up to the initials in the corner, Jessie could sense it was personal and, at least at the time it had been sent, important.

She sat down on the bed, unsure of whether to open it. She knew James had lived another life while he was away. She knew he had never filed for a divorce so she assumed that meant he had never married again, at least legally, but she had never asked him about what things had been like for him while he was so far away. In the years they had been together since he had returned, they had not spoken of the time they were apart. They had not discussed whether they dated or whether one of them had fallen in love with someone else. They had not talked about their lives as single people, and neither of them had confessed to anything more than their lonesomeness for the other.

She turned the letter over and over in her hands. It could be nothing, she thought. It could be a newspaper clipping sent to him from an old friend. It could be a letter telling of birth or death or even something about a happening in Hope Springs. But she would never know unless she opened it to read it. And opening other people's mail was never the way of Jessie Jenkins. She did not snoop. She did not busy herself with the activities and happenings of her friends and family unless she was invited into the situation.

Like most folks her age, born in the Depression era, Jessie had grown up poor in a house with too many children, and since they never had much of anything, no bed of their own, no new toys or store-bought clothes, not enough food, never extra coats or winter clothes, they valued the things they did have. They valued honesty and loyalty, hard work and respect. Her parents could not give their children material things but they had made sure they handed them down the things that matter most. And staying out of other people's affairs, letting private things stay private, had been a lesson Jessie had learned at a very early age.

She got up from the bed and placed the letter on the dresser next to an ashtray that James used to empty his pockets every night. She decided to keep at her chore of spring cleaning. She pulled out everything from under the bed, assessed what needed to stay there and what could be put in the attic or taken to Goodwill. She straightened the blankets and quilts in the trunk, and started in on the drawers where she and James kept their clothes. She arranged and folded all of his and then had moved over to the dresser where she kept her clothes, the one with the letter resting on top, when she heard the back door open and knew that James had come home for lunch.

While Jessie stayed at home, cleaning, cooking,

taking care of various and assorted grandchildren or great-grandchildren, making calls for church or for a campaign of some kind, James helped their son, James Jr., as he tried to make a living farming. Having his father around had certainly helped things, but it was still hard, and even with the second set of hands, James Jr. still had to work nights just to make ends meet.

Jessie finished folding the shirts and sorting the socks and slid the drawers back in. She glanced over at the letter and waited for James to come back to the bedroom. She heard his steps coming closer.

"Hey baby," he said as he rounded the corner and stood inside the door. "You still cleaning this room?" he asked.

"We got too much stuff," Jessie commented, and pointed to the piles of clothes and linens she was planning to bag and give away.

"It's amazing, isn't it?" he asked, shaking his head. "We grew up with one set of clothes for work and one set of clothes for Sunday church and that was all we ever needed. Now it seems like we got to have a set of clothes for every day of the week."

"More like every day of the month," Jessie added. She sat down on the bed, and James came over and sat down beside her.

"You get the ground plowed?" Jessie knew that her husband was driving the tractor that morning since he and their son were planning to start breaking and turning the soil for the spring planting.

"We got the upper field done but then the tractor just cut off and we couldn't get it started again. I think the carburetor is dirty." He glanced over at the clothes on the floor. "Did you clean out my stuff too or is that just yours?" he asked.

"That's just mine, if you can believe it," she replied. "You'll need to sort through your own stuff since I don't know what you want to keep and what you want to get rid of."

James nodded. He looked back in front of him and saw the letter on the top of the dresser. "What's that?" he asked, and leaned up to get a closer look.

"Fell off the shelf in the closet," Jessie answered. "I thought it might be important."

James reached for the letter and held it in his hands. He folded it and stuffed it in his front shirt pocket. It was clear to Jessie that he recognized the letter and that he didn't want to open it in front of her.

They sat in an awkward silence.

"You ready for lunch?" Jessie asked, and stood up from the bed. She brushed off the front of her blouse and pants and headed out of the room into the kitchen. Once there, she started preparing lunch for herself and James. In a few minutes he joined her.

"Leftovers okay?" she asked as she pulled dishes

from the refrigerator. They had eaten chicken and rice and a few vegetables the night before, and there was plenty for them to enjoy another meal. She opened containers and poured them into pots on the stove.

"Did you read the letter?" James asked as he eased himself into a chair at the kitchen table.

Jessie just shook her head. "You want any bread?" she asked.

"No," he answered. "No bread."

She stirred the rice and chicken together and turned up the gas on the green beans. "Tea or water?" she asked.

"Tea," he responded. "And I'll get that," he added.

Jessie nodded.

James stood up and got glasses out of the cabinet. He filled them both with ice and reached into the refrigerator and got out the pitcher of iced tea and poured both glasses full. He then placed them on the table while Jessie stood at the stove. He sat down again.

"You wanted tea, right?"

She nodded in response. Jessie kept stirring the chicken and rice, the beans, and then walked over to get plates. She seemed to have nothing else to say.

"Her name was Ramona. I dated her off and on for six years. She had a daughter by her first husband. We met at work. She was a bookkeeper. Mostly, we were just friends."

Jessie spooned out a plate full of food for each of them. She placed the plates on the table, turned off the stove, and sat down across from her husband. She closed her eyes and prayed, "Lord, for the bounty of this, thy table, we give you thanks. And may this food nourish our bodies so that we may be of greater service to you. In Christ's name, amen."

"Amen," James repeated, and lifted up his eyes to look at Jessie. She simply started eating her lunch. "Don't you want to ask me something about her?" he asked meekly.

"Her name is Ramona and she has a daughter and mostly you were friends," she recapped what she had just been told. "What else do you think I might need to know?"

James glanced down at his plate of food, picked up a fork, and took a bite. When he had swallowed, he continued. "I didn't tell you about her because I didn't see the point," he explained, even though he had not been asked.

Jessie ate a few more bites and took a drink of her tea. She wiped her mouth with her napkin. "Six years is a long time just to be friends," she noted. "Which six years were they?" she asked.

"What do you mean?" James responded.

"Which six years were they? The six years as soon as you got to D.C., the six years at the end of the time you were there, or six in the middle?"

James thought about the question. "I guess they

were the six years near the end." It appeared as if he hadn't really measured the time of when he was seeing someone else.

Jessie nodded and kept chewing.

"I didn't mean for anything to get started," he explained. "I just felt sorry, I guess, for her and her daughter, all alone like that in the big city."

Jessie looked up at her husband. "You felt sorry for her?" she asked, the anger starting to show. "You felt sorry for her and her daughter, all alone like that in the big city?"

James dropped his head.

"You left me with four children, took off without as much as a good-bye, and you found a woman in D.C. for whom you felt sorry and became her friend? Is that pretty much what you're saying?" Jessie could feel her throat tighten, and she could tell she wasn't hungry anymore.

"Our children were grown," he responded.

"The girls were fifteen and sixteen. James Jr. and Robert were barely out of high school. None of them were what I would call grown." She placed her fork down beside her plate. "And even if they were, you think I wasn't lonely or hurt or broken when you left? You think I didn't need support?"

James had no reply.

"And what kind of rationale is that anyway? You think that would somehow make it okay that you had a girlfriend? Because she was alone with a child?" Jessie shook her head, got up from the table, and emptied her plate in the trash can.

"Did you leave me for her?" she turned around and asked.

James looked up at Jessie, then he glanced away.

"Oh my God, you did! You left me for another woman? And then you came back and pretended that you missed me the whole time, that you don't know why you did what you did. I always thought it was the need to get out of Hope Springs, that you wanted to live somewhere else, but it wasn't somewhere else that pulled you out of here, it was someone else!" Jessie dropped her plate in the trash can and turned to place her hands on the sink to steady herself.

"It wasn't like that," James said as he made his way from the table to his wife. "I didn't know Ramona when I moved. I swear. I met her later, a lot of years later," he confessed. "I didn't leave you for her."

He stood behind her, waiting for something more. Jessie turned around and faced her husband. She studied him, studied his face, his eyes, trying to find the answer she knew she would never have.

"It doesn't really matter when you met her, does it?" She shook her head. "You left me and you took up with her and you didn't come back until what you had with her didn't work out. That's about it, right?" she asked.

James turned away from Jessie. He didn't reply

right away, and then it was as if he wanted to say something more, explain in some new way, and then suddenly realized it was futile. He nodded. "Yes, if you put it that way, I suppose that's about it."

"All this time and we never talked about your years away. I thought I could get past it all. I guess I thought you were in D.C. pining for me and just not able to make your way home. I don't know." She stopped, turned to the sink, and looked out the window, and then turned back to her husband.

"But now this. Now, finding out you weren't alone." She blew out a long breath. "I can't be with you right now. I just can't."

Jessie pushed him out of the way, grabbed her coat and purse, and headed out the back door.

"Jessie, wait," he called out to her, but she was already out the door.

James watched her leave. He pulled out the letter and considered calling Louise or Beatrice to let them know what had happened, but then thought better of it. He knew that Jessie would handle this in her own way.

Red Chile Chocolate Chip Cookies

¾ cup margarine or butter (1½ sticks)
1 cup brown sugar
½ cup sugar
2 eggs
1 teaspoon vanilla
dash salt
1½ tablespoons red chile powder
⅓ cup cocoa
½ teaspoon baking soda
2 cups flour
1½ cups chocolate chips

Preheat oven to 350 degrees. Mix first 8 ingredients on low speed of mixer or by hand until just blended. Mix in baking soda and flour. Mix in chips. Line cookie sheets with parchment paper. Scoop dough into small bite sizes (1 tablespoon) and bake for 8 to 10 minutes. Makes 3 dozen.

—Barb Hively, Cravin' Cookies

Chapter Thirteen

Charlotte watched from the front window as Donovan got out of his car. He was wearing jeans and a long-sleeved black Western-style shirt. He had on his boots, the black ones with the small gold plate at the toes. He walked over to the passenger's side of the car, opened the door, and cleared off the seat. He took papers and a ball cap and put them in the back. Charlotte smiled as he dusted off the seat and then closed the car door. There was something tender, she noticed, about the way he was preparing for her to join him.

He walked toward the front door, and Charlotte moved away from the window so that he wouldn't see that she had been watching him. She waited until he rang the doorbell before opening the door.

"Hey," she said, her heart beating a bit faster than it had been a few minutes earlier.

"Hello," he said in response.

Charlotte stood inside the door and he walked in, going just a few steps inside while she shut the door and moved in front of him. Their dates were still polite and still a bit awkward. "You want something to drink before we go, a soda or tea or something?" she asked.

"No, I'm good," he responded.

The two of them stood without speaking for what

seemed way too long to Charlotte, and suddenly she could feel her hands start to sweat. She wiped them on her pants legs. "Well, let me just get my purse and we can go." She walked past him, heading for the bedroom.

"You may need a heavier jacket too," he called to her.

"Oh, okay," she responded, wondering where he was taking her that required a heavy jacket. She assumed her long-sleeved blouse and sweater would be warm enough for the spring evening.

She walked into the bedroom to get her coat. She paused for a few seconds in the hallway just to try and catch her breath. She was surprised at how nervous she was. They had been out a couple of times since Carla came to the shelter, and even with the awkward way they were with each other, especially knowing that his ex-wife seemed to know every time they went out, Charlotte had felt as if the two of them were growing closer. She had enjoyed her time with Donovan so much over the previous few weeks, she found herself showing signs of the falling-in-love syndrome that she had heard the women from the shelter talking about, signs she had never really experienced before.

Darlene kept telling her that she had that "youthful glow" about her. Iris teased her about sporting a new hairstyle and wearing lipstick. Maria just watched her carefully, calling her out when she seemed distracted, occasionally making comments that Charlotte was not being prudent or careful enough. Even his ex-wife, Carla, seemed to enjoy the budding romance, telling Charlotte from time to time some of the things she remembered Donovan enjoyed.

"Don't take him to the theater," she commented once after supper when she had heard from the other women that Charlotte was going out with him. "He hates that," she added.

Charlotte was uncomfortable with getting advice from her date's ex-wife, but since she was a client, she wasn't sure how to talk to Carla about her discomfort, so she just let her say the things she wanted to say and offered no response.

Charlotte denied being different when the women teased her, but deep down, she did feel unlike she ever had before. She felt more alive, and oddly more aware of little things she had never noticed before. One day she found herself staring at the tiny yellow flowers blooming behind the shelter near the garage, flowers she had never seen in seasons before. She noticed the way water felt falling across her shoulders in the shower, never really having felt water before. For the first time, she seemed to taste the taste of sweet things. Colors seemed brighter, and she felt as if she had more energy than she had had in a long time. Never in all her imagination had she expected that beginning a relationship could be so visceral, so life-altering. She had heard all the talk of what falling in love was like but she had never really believed that having these feelings could literally change the taste of food.

Charlotte took in a breath and walked back into the front room. Donovan smiled as she stood in front of him.

"What?" she asked, uncertain of the meaning of his smile.

He shrugged. "You just look really pretty tonight," he said.

Charlotte blushed. "I look the same as I always look," she responded, pulling on her jacket. "Will this be heavy enough?" she asked. "I already packed away my big coat."

Donovan helped her pull the jacket on. "It will be fine. It's just a little chilly where we're going and I didn't want you to get cold."

"So, where are we going?" she asked as she held open the door for him to walk out first.

"It's my favorite place for dinner," he replied, sounding mysterious.

The two of them headed down the front steps, and he held open the car door as she sat down inside.

"Am I dressed okay?" she asked as he got into his seat and started the engine. She was worried that if he was taking her to a fancy restaurant, she might be a bit underdressed. She looked down at her jeans.

"You're fine," he replied, and they headed down the road.

"Is this place out of town?" Charlotte asked.

He didn't answer right away, and she watched as they turned onto Highway 666 heading north toward Tohatchi. She knew that soon they would be moving through the vast Navajo Reservation that was between Gallup and Farmington, stretching east and west for many miles. She could see that her question was being answered as the car headed out of Gallup.

"We're going to a special place from my youth. I want you to see the sun set from my perspective," he replied finally.

"Are we going to Chaco Canyon?" she asked, thinking that it was in the direction they were heading. Charlotte knew that Chaco Canyon was a new national park and on Navajo land. She had visited there when she first moved into the area, researching the stories of the early inhabitants and enjoying a day of hiking and sightseeing at the pueblo ruins and petroglyphs. It had been one of her most favorite places she had visited since living in New Mexico.

"No, we're not going that far north," he answered.

Charlotte glanced around at the old hogan villages, home to many Navajo people. "Is this where you grew up?" she asked, never having heard exactly where his home had been.

"Around these parts," he replied. "I'll take you to meet my family sometime soon," he added.

Charlotte smiled. She had wondered if the time would ever come for her to meet his family. She wondered how meeting family members worked for people in their middle years. She knew it was a part of the natural order of deepening relationships for young people, but she wasn't sure for folks after they reached a certain age. She found herself getting anxious thinking about the occasion of meeting Donovan's family and then tried shaking off her nerves since she realized that wasn't where they were heading.

They drove north for about half an hour before he turned off onto a dirt path, going west. "Hold on because this is going to be bumpy," he explained. They drove for another ten or fifteen minutes until the dirt path stopped at what appeared to be a large but empty creek.

"This is Nakaibito." He turned off the engine and opened his door. Charlotte reached for the handle and opened hers as well. "Mexican Springs," she heard him say.

Charlotte assumed he was referring to the name of the little village they had passed just before turning on the dirt path and heading to the creek.

"I used to come out here all the time when I was a boy, watching hawks, tracking coyotes. There are about four different washes that come through here. When they were dry I'd walk them all and dig along the sides for old bones and fossils. You can go for miles in these washes."

He waited until Charlotte was out and standing beside him. He pointed to two hills standing side by side to the west of where they had parked. "That's Twin Buttes," he explained. "We're standing at the southern tip of the Chuska Mountains. I grew up on the northern ridge, near the Arizona border, Sanostee," he added. "My family is spread out all along this part of the reservation. From Shiprock to Window Rock, you'll find someone from my clan." He stopped, and Charlotte looked all around her, miles and miles of desert.

"My mother's parents were from the northern part of the territory. My father's are the ones from this part. Many of my cousins live round here."

Charlotte followed his gaze back in the direction they had just come.

"We took the last name Sanchez after the Spanish arrived. But we tend to honor each other more by the clan from which we came than from a last name given to us by the government." He paused.

"My mother is from the Turtle Clan but we have family in many of the other clans as well. I went to school in Gallup, came home only for vacations and summer." He shielded his eyes and looked westward. "I swore at the beginning of every summer that I wasn't going back to the city for school, but by September, I always did."

Charlotte glanced at Donovan. She wondered about his childhood and how difficult it must have been to be shipped to school so far away. Her growing-up years had never been easy, but at least she was always close to home as a child in school. At least she lived with her mother and sister year round. "How long have you lived in town?" she asked.

"Most of my adult life," he replied. "After high school, I took the community college classes in criminal justice. I had planned to come back here and be a policeman for the tribe but I was offered a job in Gallup, so I took that." He wiped his forehead. "And that's where I've been ever since."

He turned to Charlotte. "That's where I live." He stopped for a second and looked back across the horizon. "In the city, I mean. But this, this land, this desert with her washes and canyons and tall stone faces, this is home."

Charlotte looked around her. The sun was starting to set, and with that change in the sky and land, she could immediately see why Donovan loved this place for this time of the day. It was truly magical, the horizon growing redder and redder, the hills in the distant background, the shadows lengthening all around them. For miles and miles there was not another living person. She could hear the distinct call of crows and the evening breeze dancing through the tiny new leaves on the cottonwoods. Off in the distance she heard a dog barking, but there was nothing else. It was the most quiet she had ever experienced.

"My growing up was nothing like yours," she said to Donovan. He turned to her to listen. "I grew up in small, cramped apartments on noisy streets down south." She hesitated, remembering what her early life had been like.

"Not in the city, really," she explained, "just in loud places." She leaned back against the car. "At night I used to pull my pillow over my head just trying to find some quiet." She shook her head. "There were drunks fighting on the streets beneath us, televisions blaring in the next apartment, children crying, people arguing. I tried and tried to make quiet for myself but I never found any." She closed her eyes and drew in a long breath. "This, this quiet, is what I longed for my entire life," she explained.

Donovan waited for just a minute and then walked around the car and opened the trunk. He pulled out a blanket and a large basket. While Charlotte watched he walked away from the car and spread the blanket by the edge of the wash, under a large tree. He waved her over while he began emptying out the basket.

"What's this?" she asked, walking over to where he had placed the blanket.

"This is the special place I told you about," he replied. He pulled out grapes and wild plums, a huge piece of cheese, large round slices of bread, a small bag of cookies, and a bottle of wine.

Charlotte sat down.

"Welcome to my favorite place for dinner," he said with a smile. He opened the bottle of wine and poured a glass for Charlotte, handing it to her.

"I don't drink too much," she said, taking the wine.

"I understand," he responded. "I don't either. But I thought we could enjoy a glass just for tonight," he added.

Charlotte nodded and took a sip. It was sweet, and it warmed her throat as she swallowed. She reached for a plum and took a bite.

Donavan watched as the juice spilled down her chin. He leaned over and wiped it off with his hand. He slid his thumb across her cheek and held her chin in his hand. Suddenly he leaned over and kissed her, and Charlotte started to feel dizzy. When he pulled away, she could feel her face start to redden. She quickly turned away, hoping he didn't see her blush. She cleared her throat and took another sip of wine.

"I'm sorry," he said, thinking he had acted too swiftly, noticing Charlotte's discomfort.

"No," she responded quickly. "Don't be sorry," she added. "I'm just . . ." She searched for the right words. "I just don't have a lot of experience in this kind of thing," she confessed.

"And what kind of thing might that be?" he asked. "Picnics?" he teased.

She smiled. “Kisses and wine,” she explained.

Donovan nodded. “Don’t let the setup fool you,” he responded. “I don’t have so much experience myself.”

Charlotte ate the rest of her plum and then placed the large pit on a napkin in front of whcrc shc was sitting. “You’ve been married.”

Donovan glanced up at her. It seemed as if her remark had caught him off guard. And yet, as startled as he was at the comment, he knew, as did Charlotte, that eventually they were going to have to discuss his ex-wife and their relationship.

“True,” he responded. “But that was a long time ago, and it was different for me and Carla,” he added. He took out a pocket knife, cut off a piece of cheese, and reached for a piece of bread. He handed them both to Charlotte and then did the same for himself.

“Different how?” Charlotte asked, taking his offering. She was not sure of what he meant, but glad finally to be talking about his former marriage.

“I don’t know,” he replied. “I mean we were young and it just seemed like it was my body directing everything that happened, more than my mind or my heart.” He ate the cheese and bread and swallowed. “We were sixteen when we met, the hormones were raging, if you know what I mean.”

Charlotte nodded. She took a couple of bites as well.

"We got married when we graduated from high school."

Charlotte didn't respond. She already knew that.

"She was pregnant," he added, and that information completely caught Charlotte off guard.

"You have a child?" she asked, swallowing hard, feeling as if this news somehow changed things even though she wasn't sure how at the moment.

Donovan shook his head. "The baby died," he replied. "It was born too early," he added.

"I'm sorry," Charlotte responded, not knowing what else to say.

Donovan shrugged and took a sip of his wine. "It was really harder on Carla," he acknowledged. "I was a kid and stupid. I didn't know too much."

Charlotte didn't say anything.

"Anyway, the years and the differences between us, mostly me being a police officer, the loss of the baby, it was all just more than our youthful marriage could stand. So, we broke up."

Charlotte took another drink of her wine and could feel the alcohol taking its effect on her. She was light-headed and knew that she should eat a little more. She reached over for another piece of bread and in doing so, knocked over her glass, spilling the rest of her wine on the blanket. "Oh no," she yelled, jumping up and trying to clean the mess with the napkins from the basket.

"It's okay," Donovan said, reaching over and wiping up the spill. "It's no big deal," he added.

Charlotte sat back down. "I'm sorry," she said.

"It's nothing," he responded, picking up the wet napkins and dropping them in the basket. "You're just a lightweight when it comes to alcohol, and I now know how to take advantage of you."

Charlotte smiled, hoping that the light from the sky had faded enough so that maybe he couldn't see how red she knew her face had become. She cleared her throat. "And you never dated after Carla?" she asked, returning to the conversation they were having before she spilled her drink.

He shook his head. "Well, a couple of times, but nothing ever worked out, so I became very involved in my work and I learned how to enjoy spending a lot of time by myself."

"Coming out here?" Charlotte asked.

"Coming out here," he replied.

"And I'm the first woman you've brought to Nakaibito?"

Donovan smiled at Charlotte, pleased to hear that she had already learned the correct pronunciation of the little village. "I brought a family friend, Lucinda," he confessed. "Here, have a cookie. A friend of mine has a little bakery in Albuquerque called Cravin' Cookies. These have a bite of chile at the end. I think you'll like them."

Charlotte waited with interest, taking a bite of the cookie he handed her. "The girl you brought here, was she a girlfriend?" Charlotte asked, and then stopped. “Wow!” she said in surprise. “This is a good cookie!”

“Told you,” he noted. “And the girl I brought here.” He paused. “She’s four.” He smiled.

Charlotte reached over and punched him on the leg.

“Ouch,” he yelled, and then laughed.

“But then why do you suppose I’m the one?” Charlotte asked. “Why now do you find yourself interested in me?” She finished the cookie and reached for her glass of wine.

Donovan considered the question as he poured some more wine for them both and handed Charlotte her glass. It was quiet for a while as Charlotte waited for his response, taking a sip. She listened to the evening sounds around them.

“My grandmother always said that love is a bit like seeds in the earth.” He glanced down at the big plum pit she had placed on the blanket. “Some fall and sprout right away, growing into their plants or trees not long after having been dropped. But some seeds can remain barren for many seasons, tossed by the wind, blown beneath roots of trees or hidden under stones or pushed beneath the ground. They finally sprout only when the earth has tilted in the most pleasant way.” He paused and looked at Charlotte. “I guess the earth must have shifted when I wasn’t paying attention.”

Charlotte studied him. “And a seed has sprouted?” she asked.

“A seed has sprouted,” he responded. He reached over and picked up the plum pit and a bottle of water from the basket and walked around Charlotte to a small place near the wash.

Charlotte watched as he dug a hole and placed the pit inside. He poured a bit of water on it and then covered the pit with dirt. He glanced over at her and smiled. And Charlotte didn’t know if it was the wine or if the earth had truly shifted, but she was suddenly and completely starting to fall.

Party Cheese Ball

2 8-ounce packages cream cheese, softened
1 8-ounce package sharp cheddar cheese, shredded
1 tablespoon chopped pimento
dash salt
1 tablespoon chopped green pepper
1 tablespoon finely chopped onion
2 tablespoons Worcestershire sauce
1 teaspoon lemon juice
dash cayenne pepper
finely chopped pecans

Combine cream cheese and cheese, blending well. Stir in remaining ingredients except pecans. Shape into ball and roll in chopped pecans. Chill. Serve at room temperature.

—Dick Witherspoon

Chapter Fourteen

"Good Lord, Jessie, what is it?" Bea opened the back door wide and motioned for her friend to come in. "Are you hurt? Has something happened?"

Jessie didn't speak. She only walked in, her head down, her arms wrapped around her waist. Bea couldn't tell if she was sick or devastated but she could certainly see that something terrible had happened.

"Here," Bea said, hurrying over to the kitchen table, pulling out a chair. "Sit down," she said, holding the back of the chair as Jessie sat. "You need some water?" she asked frantically. "You want some tea?"

Jessie only shook her head.

"You want me to call somebody for you?" She leaned close to Jessie. "You want me to call James?"

Jessie looked up quickly. "No, don't call him."

Beatrice sat down across from her. She didn't say anything at first. She waited, knowing that Jessie would explain when she was ready. The television was blaring from the other room, and Bea wondered if she should leave Jessie to go and turn it off.

Jessie took in a breath. "It's James."

"Is he okay?" Beatrice asked.

Jessie nodded. "He's fine," she replied.

"Then what?" Beatrice wanted to know.

"James was seeing someone while he was in D.C.," Jessie said. "I found an old letter and he confessed."

Beatrice nodded. She wasn't sure of what to say. Immediately she thought of the upcoming wedding renewal service they had been planning and started to make a list in her head of whom she might need to call to cancel. She shook those thoughts from her mind, thinking it was a little early to make those plans. "What did he say?" she asked.

"That it lasted six years and that he felt sorry for her and that mostly they were just friends." She related the story her husband had told her. "He claims that the relationship started after he left me and ended before he came back."

Beatrice nodded. She tried to remember exactly when her friend's husband returned to Hope Springs. She recalled it had been for their grandson's wedding, just after Nadine's little girl had gotten hit by a car at the church. She remembered that at first Jessie had been skeptical but then later had been delighted that her wandering husband had returned. Bea also recalled that the other members of the cookbook committee had not been so quick to celebrate the homecoming and had spent a lot of time grilling her about his motives. Of course, they had all come to accept him and were pleased that the couple had reunited. They all knew how happy it had made their friend.

"I don't know why this has me so upset," Jessie said. "He was gone a long time. I don't know what I thought. On some level I had to know he was seeing other women."

"It's easy to believe what we want to believe," Bea responded. "He came back saying that he missed you, had always missed you. He made it sound a lot like he hadn't been seeing anybody else. And you've told me that you never dated while he was gone, so it makes sense to me that you thought the same thing about him." She shrugged. "I'd be mad too," she added.

"I don't know that I am as mad as I am . . . I don't know." Jessie stopped, trying to clarify exactly what she was feeling.

"Betrayed?" Beatrice asked, recalling her own emotions about her daughter's upcoming wedding. It had been almost six weeks since she had received the invitation, and even though she had been encouraged by everyone who knew her and knew what had happened, she still had not talked to Robin. She still hadn't even decided whether she was going to the wedding. Every time she thought about calling her daughter to ask for an explanation she would find herself so angry, she knew she couldn't talk without yelling. And she knew that yelling at Robin would not help matters.

"Yeah, I guess that's what I feel." Jessie dropped

her head in her hands. "Betrayed," she repeated.

Beatrice got up from the table and poured them both a glass of water. She set a glass in front of Jessie and then sat back down across from her. "What did the letter say?" she asked, recalling how her friend had found out about the affair.

Jessie glanced up. "I didn't read the letter," she replied. She picked up the glass of water and took a sip.

Beatrice appeared surprised. "You didn't read the letter?" she asked.

Jessie shook her head. "I don't read other people's mail," she responded.

"Well, that's just silly," Bea noted.

"It probably would have just made things worse," Jessie said.

"Can they be worse?"

Jessie considered the question. She shrugged in response.

Beatrice drank some of the water. "What was the postmark of the letter?" she asked. "Was it mailed recently? Did she write to him since he's been back in North Carolina?"

Jessie shook her head again. "It was old, from the nineties, mailed to his apartment in D.C.," she replied. "But it had to be important or he wouldn't have kept it."

"Probably," Bea responded. "But maybe it was important for reasons other than you think," she added.

"Like what?" Jessie asked, unsure of what her friend meant.

Bea shrugged. "Maybe it was the letter that confirmed what he had known the entire time they were seeing each other. Maybe she was saying to him what he had known on some level and had not been able to say to himself."

"And what might that have been?" Jessie asked.

"That he should be back here, that he loved you and would never be able to love anybody else. Maybe he needed to be away from you to learn that important lesson, and maybe she was the one who was able to help him see that." Beatrice smiled. She was proud of her idea.

There was a pause.

"Which movie did that scene come from?" Jessie asked.

Beatrice sighed and waved Jessie's response away. "I can come up with my own thoughts," she replied. She hesitated. "Okay, it's from a show I saw on Lifetime." She could see that Jessie was about to speak and she added quickly. "A channel that comes standard for any cable customer!" She was sure that her friend was going to goad her once again about her television financial arrangement.

Jessie laughed. "I wasn't going to say anything," she noted.

Beatrice studied her friend. "Yes, you were," she responded. "I can see it in your eyes," she added.

Jessie grinned and shook her head. "Beatrice, I

can always count on you to make me smile."

Beatrice took a sip of her water. She put down the glass and could see Louise walking up the driveway and heading to the back door. "Well, it looks like the cookbook committee now has a quorum." She stood up from the table and went to open the door.

Jessie turned to see as Louise made her way into the kitchen. "I was driving by and saw your car," she said as she entered the room. "I need to talk to both of you," she added. She glanced around at Beatrice. "What are you watching?" she asked.

The three women listened as all sorts of indistinguishable and somewhat questionable sounds were coming from the television in the other room. Beatrice hurried past her friends and immediately turned off the TV. "It was a documentary," she explained as she pulled another chair from the dining room into the kitchen.

"Yeah, right, I've heard about those kinds of documentaries," Louise noted. She took a seat. "It's called porn."

Beatrice rolled her eyes and poured another glass of water. She sat down at the table. "Jessie has discovered that James was two-timing her while he lived in our nation's capital," she summed up the conversation for her friend.

Louise turned to Jessie. She was stunned by the revelation. "That true?" she asked.

Jessie nodded. "It's true," she replied.

"Jessie, I'm so sorry," Louise said, reaching over to touch her friend on the arm. "How did you find out?" she asked.

"She found a letter," Beatrice answered for Jessie. "But she didn't open it," she added, "because she doesn't read other people's mail." She raised an eyebrow as if she was suspicious of such a choice.

"Of course she doesn't read other people's mail," Louise responded. "Most of us with any morals don't." She looked at Beatrice.

Beatrice sat back in her seat without a response.

"Well, what happened?" Louise asked Jessie. "Did you have a fight?"

Jessie took her friend's hand. "I found the letter, and when he saw it he asked me if I read it. I told him no and then he confessed. He just said he had met a woman in D.C. and that they were mostly friends but that they had been together for almost six years."

Louise didn't respond right away. She just sat with the information, trying to imagine what her friend was feeling, trying to think of the right words to say. "Are you okay?" she finally asked.

Jessie nodded. "I'll be fine," she replied. "It was just, I don't know, a shock, I guess. It's silly for me to have thought that he never dated in all that time he was away, but I guess I just didn't want to think he was with anyone else."

Louise sat back in her seat. She folded her arms

across her chest and waited. Finally she responded. "He came home," she said softly. "Whatever he did while he was away, he chose you and he came home."

Jessie smiled. "Yes, I know. But I can't help thinking that I was maybe his second choice," she responded. "Maybe he and this woman tried to make a go of it and it didn't work out and then he came home."

"Does that matter?" Louise asked.

Jessie and Beatrice both looked at her.

"I mean, he came home. And he loves you and you love him and you've been good together since he's back. You went to Africa. He took care of you when Margaret died. He loves his children, loves his grandchildren, loves that little girl Hope. He is a big help to James Jr. He makes you happy, Jess. Does the other part really matter?"

Jessie looked away. She thought about the time she and James had shared together since he had returned to Hope Springs. She remembered how satisfied she felt having him back home, how complete she was once again. She thought about how deeply he grieved with her and for her when Margaret was dying, how he doted on the children, how he doted on her. Maybe Louise was right, she thought, maybe it didn't matter what had happened prior to his coming or what had happened that made him choose to come back. He was home, and up until she had found out this startling information, they were fine. She shook her head. "I don't know whether it ought to matter or not," she said. "But for now, it does," she said. "Honestly, I don't know why, it just does."

Louise nodded.

"You want us to jack him up?" Beatrice asked.

Louise turned to Bea. "Jack him what?" she asked.

"Jack him up," Jessie explained, laughing. "It's slang for causing him trouble," she said to Louise. "And no, Bea, I don't want you jacking anybody up."

Beatrice smiled and shrugged.

"What about you?" Louise asked Beatrice. "Have you talked to Robin?" The last time Louise had talked to Beatrice about her daughter, Beatrice had decided to call and talk to her. Louise wanted an update.

Beatrice just shook her head. "I'm still too mad. I think I'm okay about it and then I just start crying again." She sighed. "I guess Jessie and I feel a little bit the same. We've both been betrayed by the people we love. It just hurts and it takes a little while to move beyond it," she added.

"Beatrice, it's been almost two months. She's probably waiting to hear from you," Louise noted. "Have you at least decided to go to the wedding?" she asked.

Beatrice drank down the rest of her water. "I don't know," she said when she finished drinking.

She wiped her mouth. “It’s a lot of money to travel there. Dick and I aren’t rich,” she said. “Besides, if she had really wanted me to be there, she would have asked for my help in planning the wedding.”

Louise and Jessie looked at each other. They had been so hopeful that their friend had made things right with her daughter.

It was clear that Beatrice didn’t want to discuss her issues any longer, and so she turned to Louise. “What is your big news?” she asked, remembering what Louise had said when she walked into the house. “Did you finally tell George to take a flying leap?”

Louise looked first at Beatrice and then at Jessie. She took in a big breath. “No, I told him yes, I will marry him, and I’m moving to Maryland this weekend.”

Chile Cheese Samples

½ stick margarine
dash salt
pepper to taste
dash onion salt
dash cayenne pepper
¼ pound cheddar cheese, shredded
1 cup plain flour
1 cup rice cereal
1 4-ounce can green chiles, chopped and drained

Preheat oven to 350 degrees. Mix the first seven ingredients, cutting them as when making a pastry. Add the rice cereal and form into small balls. Place a dent in each ball. Place them on a lightly greased cookie sheet and fill each small dent with chopped green chiles. Bake for 12 to 15 minutes.

—Maria Roybal

Chapter Fifteen

"Maria, just tell her it's an emergency." Beatrice had called Charlotte to ask for her help to stop Louise from marrying George.

"Mrs. Witherspoon, I have explained to you that Charlotte is in an important meeting. She's trying to get placement for a resident." Maria was answering the phones while Charlotte was taking a meeting with a county social worker. They were in the dining room of the shelter, which also served as the conference room.

"What is this *Mrs. Witherspoon* stuff? Maria, this is Beatrice. Knock that professional mess off."

"Bea, I can't interrupt the meetings," she said.

"Wait! Is it her boyfriend's ex-wife?" Beatrice wanted to know. "It's about time!" she added. "That woman needs to go on with her life somewhere other than with Charlotte."

Maria cringed when she heard the question and remarks. Beatrice had found out about Carla and her relationship with Charlotte's boyfriend even though Maria had never intended to tell anybody who was staying at the shelter. Carla had answered the phone one of her first days as a resident, and the call had been from Beatrice. Somehow in that conversation, Beatrice had pushed Carla for information about Charlotte and Charlotte's new boyfriend. In her next call to the shelter, Beatrice had talked to Maria, and somehow, information about the woman Beatrice had been talking to earlier had just slipped from Maria.

Maria had confessed what happened to Charlotte, understanding that she had overstepped professional boundaries. Without giving out names, she had identified one of the residents to an outsider. She was mortified with her behavior and had even tendered her resignation as a volunteer. Charlotte had convinced her to withdraw that resignation and not to worry about it. "Beatrice," she had said to the volunteer, "is a big mouth, but she's two thousand miles away and she would never do anything to harm Carla or anyone else."

Maria, though persuaded to stay and to forgive herself, was still upset about what had happened, and when Beatrice reminded her that she knew about Carla, Maria just wanted the phone conversation to end. *"Señor, perdóname,"* she said.

"Oh, for heaven sakes, Maria," Beatrice responded. "The Lord doesn't need to forgive you anymore. I'm not going to say anything to anybody about who is staying at the shelter. I've already promised you that! Besides, the girl was the one who told me her name, not you."

Maria sighed. She knew that Charlotte had to tell Carla not to answer the office phones and not to reveal her identity to anyone. "I will tell Charlotte that you called but I cannot interrupt the meeting," she repeated.

Charlotte had been very clear that she was never to be pulled out of a meeting or conference or even conversation to take a call from Beatrice. The "emergency" Beatrice always used as an excuse never turned out to be one.

"Thank you, Beth." Charlotte was coming down the hall. As she escorted the social worker out the back door, she passed the office.

"Okay, Beatrice, it's your lucky day. She's finished with the meeting. Hold, please." Maria hit the hold button on the phone, glad not to have to argue with Charlotte's friend any longer.

"Phone call, Charlotte," Maria called out.

"Thanks," Charlotte responded, and said goodbye to the visitor and headed back to the office.

"It's Beatrice," Maria noted.

Charlotte rolled her eyes and smiled.

"Hey Bea, what's up?" She sat down at her desk, looking over her calendar and realizing that she had three other meetings scheduled for the day. She also noticed a red heart, which meant Donovan was going to stop by her house on his way home from work.

It was Thursday and they usually ate dinner together in front of the television on that particular weeknight. They liked to watch old movies.

"Are you finding her another place to live?" Beatrice asked.

Charlotte was confused. "What are you talking about?" she replied.

"The ex. Have you found her a new place to live?"

Charlotte relaxed in her chair. "We don't discuss our clients, Beatrice, you know that."

"She needs to find another place to live is all I'm saying," Beatrice responded. She had already given Charlotte an earful for dating a policeman who had an ex-wife who was an abuse victim. Beatrice had asked a lot of questions about Carla and Donovan, and even though Charlotte never answered any of them, Beatrice had made up her mind about the situation. She thought it was very troublesome for an ex-wife of a current beau to be a client of Charlotte's.

Of course, Charlotte was all too well aware of the trouble and the complications with the arrangement of clients and boyfriends. She had talked to Carla more than she wanted to talk about her personal life, and she had heard Donovan talk more about his former marriage than she really wanted to hear. In the end, there was nothing she could do about the way things were, and even if she could change the situation, she knew that Beatrice was not the one from whom she should be receiving counsel.

"Why did you call, Bea?" Charlotte asked, hoping to change the subject.

Beatrice sighed, knowing that as hard as she might push, she wasn't going to get Charlotte to talk about her boyfriend or his ex-wife. "It's Louise," she answered. "She's going to marry Roxie's crazy sick husband."

Charlotte paused, taking in the information. She knew a little about the marriage proposal because Louise had called her weeks prior when it was first given. She also knew that Beatrice had actually supported it when George had first asked Louise. "I thought you didn't see this as a problem," she commented.

"I was stupid," she responded. "Of course it's a problem."

"Why?" Charlotte asked, glad to be on another subject.

"Because she's going to move to Maryland," Beatrice replied. "I never agreed to that part of this proposal. I thought they would live together in Hope Springs, that she'd hold his hand while he died here, in her home."

Charlotte could hear the disappointment in Beatrice's voice, and she too was surprised to hear first of all that Louise had agreed to marry the man, and now that she would leave her home for him. "Why can't he go to North Carolina?" Charlotte asked.

"Because of all of his stuff: his doctors, his house, his furniture, it's all there with him," Beatrice answered. She paused. "I think he expects Louise to help him clean everything out, sell his house, and take care of him while he dies."

"Does she say how long he has left?" Charlotte asked.

"Nobody can predict that," Beatrice replied. "But yes, she says only a few months."

"Then, Bea, she'll be back to Hope Springs before the end of the summer," Charlotte noted, thinking that since it was April then, a few months meant she would probably only be gone until August and then their friend would be back in North Carolina. It was clear to her then why Louise would agree to leave her home. "It's not permanent."

"Not permanent?" Bea responded. "That's no reason to agree to his demands."

Charlotte heard the disappointment suddenly change to anger. She could see that there was more to this conversation than just Louise going to live with George. "I don't think he made demands," Charlotte said. "Louise wants to do this," she added. "You've heard her."

"Louise is crazy," Beatrice said.

"Beatrice, Louise is not crazy. She just wants to be close to Roxie, and in her unique way of looking at things, it does bring her closer to her friend. And it sounds like she's really helping George out, so tell me, why has this got you so upset?" Charlotte asked. "Do you think she's wrong to get married for the reasons she's giving?"

There was a pause.

"No, I don't think that. I always said that marriage is about a lot of things and love is only a part of that. She deserves his money and she loves to take care of people, we all know that. I don't judge her for marrying George even though she doesn't love him. I think her reasons are sound. And I think Roxie would be completely grateful to both of them for what they are doing for each other, in her honor." She hesitated. "I'm not mad about that. The truth is . . ." She hesitated and then continued, "The truth is I just feel like my world is slipping away from me."

Charlotte didn't respond.

"Jessie and James have postponed the wedding renewal service."

Charlotte knew about that too. Jessie had called to explain, and Charlotte had completely understood. She had canceled her airline ticket until they set a new date. She had been sorry to hear the news about James and his affair, but she thought the two of them were on their way to figuring things out. She had agreed that postponing the renewal ceremony was the best idea. Jessie still harbored anger and bitter feelings about James, and it was obvious that she needed a little time. But in spite of how things were, Charlotte was confident that they would work things out.

"I know, Bea. And I know you had made a lot of plans for that event." Charlotte sounded sympathetic. She knew about the photographer and the florist and the musicians. She knew that Beatrice had given a lot of energy toward organizing details.

"I was making a cookbook," Bea said.

Charlotte smiled. Beatrice had mentioned that she was creating a special gift for the couple but she hadn't explained what it was. "A cookbook," Charlotte repeated.

"Nothing fancy. I was just gathering a few finger food recipes, wedding reception hors d'oeuvres, putting them in a little special wedding cookbook. I was adding a few cake recipes at the end, some of those that didn't get in the contest at Christmas last year. I already took it to the copy shop and they designed a real nice cover, using a picture of a big wedding cake with Jessie and James's names at the top."

Charlotte remembered the recipe contest Beatrice had organized the previous Christmas. Even she had submitted a cake recipe. "That's really special, Bea, and when they decide to have their ceremony it will still be an appropriate gift."

"But maybe they won't decide to have it. Maybe they think it's a stupid idea and they'll not do it," Bea responded.

"Then you can give it to them for Christmas next year."

There was no reply, and Charlotte realized that it sounded as if she was minimizing Bea's disappointment. "Bea, I'm sure they will have their event. They just need a little time."

"But then Louise will be gone," Bea noted. "If they have it in the summer, she probably won't come back. She's going off to Maryland to marry her best friend's husband. The world's just gone nuts. Television shows make more sense than my life."

Charlotte let her friend vent.

"Jessie's despondent. You're far away. Margaret's dead. And Robin . . ." She didn't finish the sentence.

"Robin is getting married and she invited you to the wedding." Charlotte had been included in this Hope Springs drama just like all the others. She waited and then continued. "I agree with you that it was hurtful how she did it, but she did invite you, Bea, and you need to respond to her. You need to call your daughter and talk to her."

"Yes, I know. Everybody tells me the same thing. But the truth is she should come to me. She and her Farrell Monk ought to drive themselves to my house and tell me to my face that they are getting married. It's obscene that a mother finds out that her daughter is getting married from an invitation in the mail."

Charlotte didn't respond at first. She considered how she would tell her mother if she and Donovan ever got to the place that they wanted to get married. She would never confess such a thing to anyone, but she sort of understood why Robin had handled the arrangements the way that she had. Mothers and weddings could be trouble.

She cleared her throat and pushed those thoughts aside. "I agree with you, Beatrice. What Robin did was wrong. But you can stop this pattern of non-communication before it goes on any longer. You can let her know that you are hurt by how she handled this, but you can still love her and support her as she begins her marriage."

There was no response from Beatrice, but Charlotte knew she was still on the line because she could hear her breathing.

"Beatrice, she may not say it, but she still needs her mother."

"You're right, I know you're right," she finally said. "I'm just hurt is all," she added. "You won't get married and not tell me, will you, Charlotte?" she asked.

Charlotte heard the pleading tone. "Of course I won't," she promised.

"You wouldn't invite an ex-wife to your wedding, would you?" she asked.

Charlotte considered the question. "Actually, he probably would if I didn't," she explained. "They happen to be good friends," she added. The friendship between Donovan and Carla was becoming a bit difficult for Charlotte. It was something she was trying to work through. She was listening to her advice to Beatrice, and she knew she should follow it for herself too. She needed to talk to Donovan about her feelings about his relationship with Carla.

"Well, that's not good," Beatrice commented. "Why are they such good friends?" she asked.

"Bea, I guess they share a special bond, and unfortunately, having a new girlfriend doesn't really make that bond go away," she answered.

"You aren't happy about it either, are you?"

Charlotte decided to be truthful. "I'm going to talk to him about it," she confessed.

"Hmmpff," Beatrice said. "The world has just gone crazy," she repeated. "Completely crazy," she added. "Whatever happened to a good old-fashioned church wedding between two young people in love, without ex-wives and the need to go to Mexico?"

Charlotte laughed. "I don't know, Beatrice. It's just the way of things, I guess."

"Well, that's no excuse." She sighed. "I love you, Charlotte Stewart."

"I love you too, Beatrice Newgarden Witherspoon. Give Dick a kiss." She paused. "And don't worry so much. It's going to work out fine. Give Louise your blessing as her friend. Give Jessie a little time. And give your daughter a call." She waited. "Okay?"

"Okay," Beatrice responded. And the conversation was over.

George's Dipping Dip

1 8-ounce package cream cheese, softened
4 ounces tomato sauce
1 package dry Italian dressing mix
2 tablespoons chopped green olives

Combine all ingredients until blended. Chill. Serve with chips or crackers.

—George Cannon

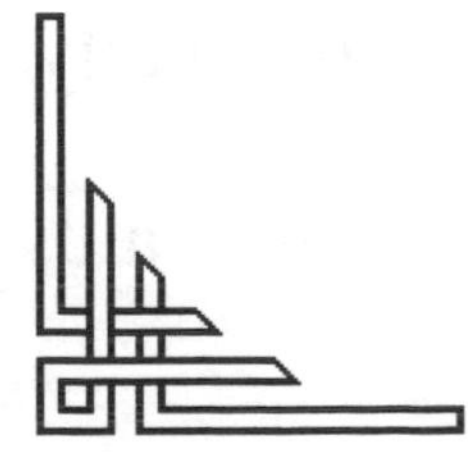

Chapter Sixteen

"This is your room." George motioned to the master bedroom. "I moved my stuff out and I've taken the smaller one in the back." He stood in the hallway as Louise walked into the room.

"I wasn't expecting to stay in here," she responded, pulling her suitcase behind her. "I would be fine in the guest room. That's where I'm used to staying." Louise had been a frequent guest in her best friend's home over the years Roxie and George had lived there.

"No, this is best for you. You'll have your own bathroom and plenty of privacy." George appeared uncomfortable. He shifted his weight from side to side, still standing at the door. "Roxie would want you to be in here," he added.

Louise turned to George. She could see how much his health had deteriorated since he had driven to North Carolina on that late winter day to propose. She guessed that he had probably lost forty or fifty pounds since his diagnosis of lung cancer. His face was gaunt and his clothes were too large. He looked like a shadow of the big man he used to be. "Yeah, she probably would," she finally said.

"I'll get your other belongings," George said, and quickly turned to leave.

Louise was going to tell him that she would get her things herself, that he needed to rest, but when she glanced at where George had been standing, he was gone. She sighed. They had driven in from North Carolina just a few hours before and had gone straight to the courthouse when they arrived in town. They had been married for about an hour. Louise was also tired, and she sat down on the bed. She looked around the room.

Roxie was everywhere. George hadn't changed a thing since he had been married to her. All the knickknacks she had purchased, all the same linens. Even her old jewelry box was still on the top of the dresser. Louise wondered if George had cleaned out anything since Roxie's death.

The curtains were the same ones Roxie made when they first moved into the house. Louise remembered when she purchased the material. Louise had come up to visit and help them move in, and the two women had gone together to buy window treatments and new linens as well as other supplies. The two friends had spent many hours getting the house decorated and suited to Roxie's ideas.

After seeing what the stores were offering, Roxie had decided to make her own window treatments, and the two had driven to every fabric store in a one-hundred-mile radius of the couple's new home. Roxie finally settled on a nice floral fabric, and she had bought every yard the store had in stock. She had sewn long, thick curtains, and even after more than forty years of hanging in the same windows, they still looked new and fashionable. Louise stood up and walked over to the window. She touched a curtain, pulling it away from the glass. When she did, she could see outside in the front of the house, and she noticed George struggling with the other suitcases. She was going to go outside and help him and then she waited. She decided just to watch. He pulled one out from the backseat slowly, set it down beside him, and then leaned against the car. It was obvious that he was struggling. Finally, he pulled out the other one and stopped again.

Louise let the curtain fall back and returned to the bed and sat down. "What on earth am I doing here?" she asked herself. She glanced down at her left hand. She was wearing a wedding band, one that Bea and Jessie had bought for her to have for the civil ceremony. It was simple, just a gold band that they had purchased at the local jewelry store. "I am a married woman," she said, shaking her head. "I am gay and married to my best friend's dying husband."

She thought about the events of the last few days. The good-bye lunch she had with her friends that later turned into a silly bridal shower they had organized at Lester's, complete with lingerie and the giving of the ring they had picked out. Beatrice had even ordered a special cake for Louise, pink frosting with a little bride standing on top. They had invited some of their church friends to attend. Even the pastor showed up, although it was clear that he was uncomfortable at the gathering and with the whole notion of Louise marrying George. He said a quick blessing and soon departed.

Louise remembered how James made an appearance as well and how awkward he had been around Jessie. It seemed as if they hadn't been around each other in a number of weeks and they acted clumsy and fidgety around each other. Jessie moved to the opposite side of the diner when he arrived. James had brought a gift, a set of note cards, already addressed and stamped, half made out for Bea and half for Jessie. He had given Louise the gift, looked around the diner, found Jessie's glance, nodded at her, and left.

After Jessie found out about the other woman and had confronted her husband, James had moved in with his son, and even though he and Jessie still talked to each other, it was obvious to everyone that something painful had happened between them.

Louise was worried about her friends. She even asked Jessie if she wanted her to stay in Hope Springs, offering to cancel the wedding and the move for her friend, but Jessie had convinced her that there was nothing that Louise could do and that she needed to go forward with her life.

"My life," Louise said to herself, dropping her

head in her hands. "This is some life," she added.

"Are you sorry you've come?" George was standing at the door. He surprised Louise.

She snapped up her head. "No," she said. "I was just thinking about Jessie and James," she acknowledged. "They're having problems."

"Yeah, you mentioned the affair." He stood at the door. "Are you sure it's just that and not all this?" he asked.

Louise decided to be honest. "It is just a little crazy, don't you think?" she asked.

George rolled the suitcase into the room and placed it beside the other one that was near the bed. He nodded toward the bed. "Can I sit?" he asked.

"Yes, of course," Louise replied, moving over to make room for him to sit beside her.

He sat down. His breathing was short and labored.

"You okay?" Louise asked. "You want a glass of water or something?" She started to get up.

George just shook his head, holding up his hand, to wave away the offer.

Louise sat back down. She slid her hands down the front of her legs, resting them on her knees. She waited.

"Roxie loved this room," she finally commented. She glanced around. "She had everything exactly like she wanted it." She noticed the color of the paint, the carpet, the design of the bedspread.

"She always said that the bedroom should be a person's sanctuary, a place where everything was restful and relaxing." Louise shook her head. "She read all of these books, did all of this research, picking the colors and the fabrics to be soothing and calming. She was determined to create a gentle space for the two of you."

George smiled. "She had this room painted three times before she found the exact color of blue she had in mind." He reached in his back pocket and took out a handkerchief. He wiped his forehead. "I kept saying to her the colors all looked the same. What is the big deal? And she'd say, 'this one is just too dark, too stormy. I want light blue, I want morning sky blue, not noon sky blue.' "

Louise smiled. "She was particular about her paint colors. That's for sure."

"She was particular about a lot of things," George noted.

Louise nodded. "The foods she fed her family, her Christmas cards, how she dressed. I always felt like such a slob around her because she was so perfect in everything she presented, everything she did. And she never seemed to be burdened by all those things. She was also so light and carefree and still managed to make everything perfect." She paused. "I've never been like that."

"She used to tell me that she wished she could be more like you," George commented.

Louise turned to George with surprise. "How so?" she asked.

"She thought you were the smartest person she knew. She always thought no one took her seriously because she was so unfettered by life and because she liked being a homebody. She liked to cook and plan meals and sew. She thought you were more of a real woman because you had a career and read a lot of books and because you could argue so well with me. You could always make your points so clearly." George looked at Louise. "She thought she was never quite smart enough."

"Well, that's about the silliest thing I ever heard," Louise responded.

George shrugged. "That's what she said."

The two of them sat on the bed, side by side.

"What do you think she would say about this—" Louise stopped, trying to find the right words.

"Arrangement?" George interrupted.

Louise nodded.

He paused. "I think she would approve." He turned to Louise. "Don't you?" he asked. "You knew her better than I did," he added.

This comment surprised Louise. "You really think that?" she asked.

George dropped his hands in his lap. "Of course I think that." He took in another breath. His breathing seemed to be under control again. "After we got married, she always said that she wished she was living with you instead of me, that the two of you made better roommates than we did and that she didn't have to tell you everything she was thinking like she did to me."

Louise scratched her chin. She smiled. "It's just a woman thing, I guess." She lightly punched George in the side with her elbow.

"I knew I could never come between the two of you," he commented.

"It wasn't like you didn't try," Louise responded. "You never liked me, did you?" she asked.

George considered the question. "I was just jealous," he replied. "I always knew you were the one she wanted to talk to about everything. You could always make her laugh, always make her feel better." He coughed. "If I remember correctly, you never cared for me either."

Louise nodded. "You took my best friend away," she said. "How was I ever supposed to like you after that?"

George smiled. "But somehow Roxie made us get along."

"She was the peacemaker," she noted. "Those women at the mill could fight like cats and dogs, and Roxie would always find a way to ease the tensions, bring them together to be friends. She was good at that," Louise added.

George nodded. "She was good at a lot of things," he said. "But you didn't answer your own question."

"What's that?" Louise asked, forgetting about the earlier part of the conversation.

"What do you think she would say about us?" he asked.

Louise shrugged. "I think she would want you to be happy, that she would say that she was glad that someone she trusted was taking care of you, looking after you, being with you."

"Is that the only reason you're here?" George asked. "The reason you married me?"

Louise paused. "It's the main reason," she answered. "I'd do anything for Roxie," she added.

"Even marry her sorry old husband?"

Louise shrugged. "I guess that's what I did."

George nodded, wiped his forehead again, and then placed the handkerchief back in his pants pocket.

"Do you think she could ever forgive what I did to her?" he asked.

Louise turned to George. She understood that he was referring to the affair he had during the last year of Roxie's life. She didn't answer right away. She recalled how her friend had never spoken a harsh word about her husband. In those rare moments of clarity after she had moved in with Louise, her Alzheimer's in full-blown status, she simply made comments that she had hoped that George was okay, and the only disappointment she had ever named was that his actions had caused an estrangement with their children.

Louise knew that she had never spoken of him in anger or shown any signs of bitterness toward him. She had often wondered how much Roxie knew about the affair, whether she simply chose not to consider it, act like it hadn't happened, but in the end she knew that Roxie did know and that in some inexplicable way, she had not gone to her grave with any resentment or harbored any ill will toward her husband.

"She already has forgiven you," Louise replied. "She forgave you before she died," she added.

George's eyes filled with tears. "I was wrong to do what I did. I'm sorry for that, been sorry a long time. She didn't deserve that."

"No, she didn't," Louise responded.

There was a pause.

"Is that why you married me?" Louise asked. "Are you trying to make amends with Roxie for what you did by marrying me and giving me all of your worldly goods, her worldly goods?"

George thought about the question. "Mainly, yes, I guess so."

Louise nodded, thinking about the answer. "Well, we are some pair, aren't we?" she asked, punching George again in the side. "She's probably just laughing at the two of us, old and ornery and together."

"Still the peacemaker, I'd say," George responded.

"Still the peacemaker," Louise repeated.

There was a pause in the conversation, and George slapped his leg and stood up. “Well, I’ll let you get settled. I’m going to go see what I can rustle us up for supper,” he noted.

“Thank you, George,” Louise said, looking up at her new husband.

“Thank you, Louise.” And he headed out of his bedroom, leaving Louise to make herself at home.

Smooth Sanchez Dip

1 medium onion, chopped
1 large ripe avocado, cut in small pieces
1 medium tomato, chopped
6 large green chiles, roasted, peeled, and chopped
4 ounces pimento cream cheese
½ teaspoon cumin
½ teaspoon onion salt
pinch salt
dash pepper

Mix all ingredients in blender and blend until smooth. Serve with chips or crackers.

—Donovan Sanchez

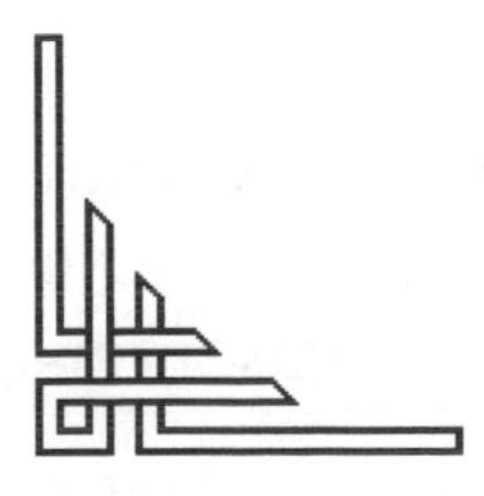

Chapter Seventeen

Charlotte watched from the front door of the shelter as Donovan helped Carla into the front seat of his car. He was smiling at his ex-wife as she grabbed him around the neck, pulling him closer to her as she sat down. He said something to her, she laughed, and he shut the door. He walked around the car and was getting in on his side when he looked up at Charlotte briefly, like it was an afterthought, waved, and dropped down in his seat and shut his door. He was still smiling when they drove away. Donovan was taking Carla to a doctor's appointment and then driving her to visit her mother somewhere out of town. She planned to stay with her family for a few days.

Donovan's ex-wife was doing much better physically, and Charlotte was hopeful that this trip meant she would be moving out soon. There were discussions about possible living situations for her, including moving back home with her parents. Carla had more options of places to stay than most of the women at St. Mary's. She had family members who were willing to take her in and several friends who had even asked her to come live with them. Charlotte had spoken to Carla about these possible residential options, but Carla was noncommittal and reported that she preferred staying at the shelter.

Charlotte hadn't wanted to admit it but she was getting a little perturbed with her resident. She was pushing Carla to find housing as soon as possible. The two of them had already had a couple of intense conversations because Carla had broken a number of shelter rules. She had brought a friend into the home, she had not carried out her assigned tasks to clean and cook, and she had confessed to taking phone calls at the shelter from her husband while he was in jail. Charlotte had expressed to Carla before she left that she was hopeful that this trip would help Carla find clarity about where she was moving next. Charlotte was losing patience with her and the entire situation.

Maria was standing beside Charlotte, watching as well. When the car pulled out, she made a kind of clucking sound and turned aside, walking away.

"What does that mean?" Charlotte called out, shutting the door.

Maria turned back around. "It means nothing," she replied.

"Oh, come on, you know you meant something with that noise." Her voice had a ring of irritation in it.

Maria shook her head. *"Pobre la mujer que no se da cuenta de lo que pasa debajo de su propios ojos."*

"English, Maria," Charlotte barked.

"He and his ex-wife are too close," she said. "And you should put a stop to it," she added. She headed down the hall. "And she needs to find another place to live."

"What do you think I should—" Charlotte stopped. She realized that she was talking much louder than she usually did. She remembered that the newest resident, a young pregnant woman who had arrived the previous night, bruised and scared, was napping in one of the bedrooms. She followed Maria. "What do you think I should do?" she whispered.

Maria walked into Charlotte's office and took a seat across from the desk. Charlotte walked around her desk and sat down in her chair.

Maria shook her head. "I don't know," she replied. "But you can't keep acting like this friendship is fine with you. It's obvious to me and to everyone else that you're bothered by this."

"Who is everyone else?" Charlotte asked. She figured the women in the shelter had been talking about her relationship with Donovan when she wasn't around, and that bothered her almost as much as Carla's friendship with her boyfriend.

"Iris, Darlene, Gilbert," Maria replied.

"Gilbert?" Charlotte asked. "You've told Gilbert?"

Maria waved the question away. "Gilbert already knew before I told him anything. He saw your starry eyes the first time he saw you look at the police officer." She touched the sides of her hair. "Gilbert misses nothing when it comes to *cosas del amor*, matters of the heart," she translated.

"He also said that it was bad business for Donovan to spend so much time with his ex-wife." She hesitated. "This he knows because he sees them at church together, not because I say anything to him at home." She placed her finger against her lips, demonstrating her determination not to break confidences ever again.

"They were high school sweethearts," Charlotte explained. "They were married. They're friends," she added.

"And she relies too much on him," Maria pointed out. "And he sees no problem with that."

"He's helping her through a bad situation," Charlotte rationalized.

"He's meddling in another family's business," Maria countered. "It isn't good for him and it isn't good for her. And if her husband finds out, it won't be good for anyone." She crossed her legs, smoothing down the front of her dress. "Isn't that part of the reason she's here in the first place? Wasn't he jealous of her first husband?" She sat up tall in her chair. "Maybe he had reason to be jealous?"

Charlotte didn't answer. She leaned her head against the back of her chair. She knew that all these things Maria was saying were things she had already told herself. She had even tried to talk to

Donovan about her concerns about his friendship with Carla. She warned him about being too close to her and how that might affect everything, from legal proceedings to Carla's relationship with her husband.

When she brought up her concerns, he would listen to Charlotte, appear as if he took her seriously, but then time would pass and he would never do anything about stopping his ex-wife's behavior. Carla called him every time he and Charlotte were on a date and he took every call. She asked him to run errands for her, which he did. It even seemed to Charlotte that there was a possibility that the two of them had hatched some plot to seek revenge on Carla's husband, who was soon scheduled to be released from jail. She had not asked Donovan about that because she didn't want to believe that he was capable of such a thing. And she certainly didn't want to be an accessory to illegal activity, and she wasn't sure if she would have the courage to turn him in if there were indeed such plans.

"He says that he's trying to get her settled on her own," Charlotte said to Maria. "He claims that he's helping her get a place in town, that they have some mutual high school friends who may have a room for her." She blew out a breath. "I told him that I was concerned that Carla was depending upon him too much and that she needed to make some of these decisions for herself, to have some say about her own life. I tried to explain that she needed to do that for her own self-esteem and that it would be better for her in the long run if she was able to say that she managed this time in her life on her own."

Maria rolled her eyes. "She is a user."

"Maria!" Charlotte said sharply. "She is our client and our resident," she noted. "She is a victim of domestic abuse. She deserves our nonjudgmental care."

"Señor, perdóname," she said, making the sign of the cross on her chest. "I do not mean to speak ill of a victim but she knows exactly what she's doing with your officer." She shrugged and looked away. "Even Darlene says the same thing," she added.

"Darlene says what?" Charlotte asked, already regretting her question. She tried not to participate in the women's talk that happened at the shelter. She tried to stay above the gossip and what she called "the fray." As the executive director, she liked to maintain a professional distance with all of the residents. She was extremely displeased that the women knew as much as they did about the man she was dating. Carla talked a lot about her former husband and her former marriage to all the other women, and Charlotte figured that they actually knew as much about Donovan as she did.

"She says that Carla asks her about the two of

you, where you go, what the two of you are doing, how serious it is."

Charlotte leaned forward, dropping her head in her hands. She glanced back up at Maria again. "I don't know," she finally said. "I've talked to Donovan. He doesn't seem as concerned as I do. He just tells me that there is nothing between the two of them anymore and that he knows best how to help Carla."

Maria made the clucking sound again. When she glanced over to Charlotte, her friend was glaring at her. She quickly stopped.

"Don't you have some forms to file?" Charlotte asked.

Maria stood up from her chair and turned to leave the office. "I'm sorry, Charlotte," she said. "I only want for your happiness," she added.

"I know, Maria, I just don't know what to do about this," she responded.

Maria nodded and left the room. Charlotte rested her elbows on the desk, dropping her chin in her hands. She thought about Donovan and how close they had become over the previous months. Things had started to become more and more serious, or at least that's what she had thought.

She had met his family, his parents, a grandmother, a couple of brothers. She had liked them and was happy to learn some of the Navajo traditions. She had enjoyed large family meals with them. She loved hearing their stories and laughing at their humor. She liked watching Donovan with his mother and his nieces and nephews. He was easy with them, putting aside his tough cop exterior as soon as he drove onto his parents' land. She thought they seemed to approve of her too, his mother taking her under her wing, showing her how they baked their bread in the large outdoor ovens found behind the houses on the reservation. She had not seemed annoyed or aggravated with Charlotte when she asked questions about Navajo customs or traditions. On the contrary, she seemed pleased to hear of Charlotte's interest, and she answered every question to satisfaction.

Charlotte and Donovan had talked about everything in their courtship. They had discussed their childhoods, their religious and political views, their likes and dislikes, their dreams. They had even discussed taking a trip back to North Carolina so that Charlotte could introduce him to her home and family. Everything about the relationship was moving ahead so beautifully. Everything between them was feeling ordered and lovely and right. Everything except his former marriage and his ex-wife, who seemed to grow more and more needy of Donovan as his relationship with Charlotte deepened. She was sure that he knew how she felt about Carla and how concerned she was at how much Carla called upon Donovan. Maria was wrong about that, Charlotte thought. Charlotte had been very clear about her concerns and her discontent with the relationship between the ex-spouses.

And yet, Donovan demonstrated some sense of duty toward his ex-wife, some connection that Charlotte couldn't understand and couldn't control. At first, she thought it was just a macho thing, the strong policeman taking care of the vulnerable, victimized woman. She had certainly witnessed that kind of relationship between many of the residents at the shelter and some of their protective friends or family members.

Later she thought the ongoing relationship had to do with that special bond that happens with first lovers. Charlotte knew that Donovan and Carla had been together when they were very young, and she knew that the feelings involved in a first love were very deep, the bond very strong. Both of them clearly acknowledged that they were each other's first love, and that fact was one they shared readily and easily. And first loves were hard to abandon.

Not that she knew any of that firsthand. As far as she could remember, she never really had a "first love." She had a crush on a student teacher in high school and she had fallen for a professor in college. She had dated a few guys that she'd liked but she had never really had that kind of "first love" experience that both Donovan and Carla had talked about when they referred to each other in conversations. Charlotte thought that maybe the fact that they were each other's first was the reason they were so close. She wasn't sure.

She also wondered if their connection was that they had been married and Donovan would always feel like a husband to Carla even if they were no longer together. She wondered if there was some Navajo custom of being bonded in marriage, a bond that would never dissolve no matter what happened to the relationship. Charlotte knew that Donovan believed that all beings, animal and people, were connected and that people were somehow related to each other in a way that must be honored through offering assistance and care. He had also told Charlotte that he believed that if people connected themselves to others through the sharing of stories and especially the sharing of love, then they became responsible for each other until their deaths.

At the time he had said this, early in their dating, she thought he was speaking of them and explaining that even though they didn't know each other all that well, they had shared something important and significant, and because of that, he was committed to her as his friend forever. Looking back at the conversation and thinking about it while considering his relationship with Carla, Charlotte suddenly considered the notion that he was trying to explain to her about his devotion to his ex-wife. She wondered as she sat at her desk, still aggravated at the attention he showed to

Carla, if he wasn't speaking about the two of them at all, but rather that he was really trying to justify even then his ongoing relationship with Carla.

She thought about that conversation and about his loyalty, his dedication to Carla, especially since he had brought her to St. Mary's, and wondered if they were truly divorced. She assumed that since Carla had remarried, there was evidence of a legal separation and divorce, but she wondered about an emotional break from the marriage or if there would always be a bond and connection between the two of them that she would never be able to sever.

She wondered if she was really able to be in what was beginning to feel like a polygamous relationship with Donovan. She realized that even though it would be hard to explain to anyone, she was starting to feel like a second wife to him, and that as much as she cared for him, as much as she was even starting to believe that she loved him, she was not able to be with someone who could not let go of an old lover.

Charlotte let out a long breath and knew that she was going to have to talk to Donovan soon. He was going to need to hear what she had to say. She folded her arms on the desk and dropped her head. She was sure their relationship was over.

Lana's Vegetable Dip

½ cup mayonnaise
8 ounces cream cheese, softened
½ cup small-curd cottage cheese
hot sauce to taste
salt and pepper to taste
2 teaspoons finely chopped chives

Blend first three ingredients in blender. Add hot sauce, salt and pepper. Blend until smooth. Stir in chives. Serve with vegetables, crackers, or chips.

—Lana Jenkins

Chapter Eighteen

"Oh, hello." Jessie was surprised to see James standing behind her as she grabbed the bags of groceries from the cart and placed them in the backseat of her car.

"Hey Jess," James responded. He had a couple of bags in his hand. He stood near the rear of her automobile, keeping a respectable distance.

Jessie looked around the parking lot. She noticed his car was parked not too far away from hers. "Well, fancy meeting you here," she said, placing her last bag on the floorboard and shutting the door.

"This is a small town. I'm surprised this hasn't happened before now," James noted. "Besides, it's your shopping day. And the truth is that I've been coming every Thursday morning for the last six weeks hoping I would run into you."

"Why didn't you just come by the house if you needed to see me?" she asked.

He shrugged. "I just wasn't sure I'd be well received if I just dropped by unannounced."

"So you thought running into me in the parking lot at the grocery store would give you better access?"

"Maybe," he answered.

"Well, I'm still surprised to see you," she said.

"Why?" he asked. "A man's got to eat," he explained.

Jessie unbuttoned her jacket as the sun stood high and full. "I guess I wasn't sure you'd stay in Hope Springs." She stood behind the grocery cart. "I thought you might have gone back to D.C."

James studied his wife and then dropped his head. He glanced up again. "Jessie, I love you. I'm not going anywhere. This is my home too."

Jessie nodded slowly, holding up a hand. "I know. I'm sorry. That wasn't fair. The children are glad you're around."

"No, it's fine. I deserve that. It's not your fault. And I'm not staying here for the children."

Jessie looked at her husband. It had been a couple of months since he had moved in with their son. She had seen him at church a few times. He had come by the house to pick up some of his clothes. They had run into each other at Louise's bridal shower and at a birthday party for one of their grandchildren, but except for polite greetings, they had not spoken in more than six weeks.

"I guess you're planting," she said, knowing that late spring was busy for James and their son as they made an annual attempt at farming. She thought small talk might be appropriate for this meeting. She figured she owed him that much. "The weather has been good and I guess we're past the likelihood of having another frost."

"We got the soybeans in at the end of last month.

Strawberries are about to bloom. We have more plants this year than last. The tomatoes look like they may make it, although we do need some rain." He glanced up at the sky. "They're calling for some this weekend, I heard."

Jessie nodded.

"You talk to Louise?" he asked.

"Yesterday," she answered. "George is with hospice now. He's mostly confined to a hospital bed. The nurses come twice a week. Somebody else comes to bathe and shave him regularly. A social worker has been helping them get all of his legal papers in line. He's alert and coherent when he's awake, but he's taking quite a bit of morphine for the pain. He quit eating but he will take liquids from time to time." She shook her head. "I told her that she was crazy for taking care of him but she claims that she doesn't mind. Funny, I think she really likes doing that kind of thing, even for a guy she's never cared for."

James nodded and smiled. "She's a good woman," he noted.

"The best," Jessie added.

"Have his children come to see him?" he asked. He had heard about the estrangement between George and his family. He knew that part of the reason Louise went to take care of him was that no one else would.

Jessie shook her head. "I don't think so. But I'm pretty sure Lou is working hard on that too. I figure that's part of the reason she decided to marry George, not just to take care of him but to try and help him reconcile with his family. Although I can only imagine that the two of them getting married just made things worse."

"What do you mean?" James asked.

"Well, that someone else was stepping in to take care of George, that someone had taken their mother's place, that it was Louise, Roxie's best friend, and that she's now entitled to the family wealth. It just seems too complicated to be readily accepted by his children."

James leaned against the back of the car. "Maybe," he said. "Or maybe they find some grace in recognizing that Louise has forgiven him. Maybe that helps them find a way to forgive him too. And I seriously doubt that anybody who knows Louise would think she was just doing this for the money and be angry at her for that."

Jessie nodded. "No, she's never been a gold digger, that's for sure."

"So maybe she's helping fix things for Roxie's family."

"Well, I don't see why George can't fix things for himself and his children. Why can't he just fix it?"

"Maybe he is in his own way. Maybe that's why he asked Louise to marry him, to take care of him. Maybe he knew that she could help him with that too," James commented.

Jessie glanced up, surprised.

"Maybe he knew that he couldn't make it right by himself, that he couldn't fix it by himself, so he fixed it by asking for help and thought that Louise, his wife's best friend, the godmother of his children, had all the right skills for doing what needed to be done." James shifted the grocery bags from one arm to another. "Sometimes men aren't so good at saying what they feel. Sometimes when they've made a big mistake or a couple of them, they just don't know how to fix the messes they've made. Sometimes they need help."

Jessie studied her husband. She nodded. "Well, I just hope she doesn't get herself in the middle of something terrible. Jumping into a situation like that takes more than just being able to express one's feelings."

James nodded.

Cars hurried past them, and they stopped to watch people pulling in and out of parking spaces.

"And Charlotte, how is she?"

Jessie smiled. "She's got love problems too," she replied. "Her policeman is still involved with his ex-wife, and Charlotte is having a hard time competing with a first love and the ghost of an old marriage."

"First love is hard to get around," he responded. "I don't really think it's ever possible to compete with that."

The person whose car was beside Jessie returned from the store. The couple had to move a bit closer together to get out of the way as the driver backed out and pulled away.

"Here, why don't you put your things in here?" Jessie asked, motioning to the cart she had been leaning against.

James nodded, walked closer to her, and placed his bags inside the cart. The two of them stood awkwardly near the front of her car. They both looked around them at all the activity.

"Will she stay with the guy?" James asked, referring back to Charlotte and her boyfriend. It appeared as if he didn't want the conversation to end.

"Don't know," Jessie replied.

They both noticed a friend from church walking near them. They smiled and waved.

"Is Bea going to her daughter's wedding?" he asked, recalling the family drama of Jessie's other friend and the fact that her daughter was planning to get married in Mexico. "When is that wedding again?"

"Sometime in July," Jessie answered. "And yes, I think Dick called Robin to RSVP and he went ahead and made reservations for the two of them." She blew out a breath. "I don't think Bea's spoken to her daughter yet though." She reached in her purse and took out a tissue. She wiped her nose. "What a mess it seems that we are all in."

James reached inside his jacket. He pulled out a letter.

Jessie recognized it immediately as the letter

from the woman in D.C. The letter she had found and confronted James about. The letter he had admitted came from a woman he had been in a relationship with. The letter Jessie had never read.

"I want you to read it," he said, handing it to her. "I think it would help," he added.

Jessie studied the letter, then looked back at her husband's face. She didn't reach for it. "I don't see how that could help," she said.

"Maybe it won't but I think you should read it anyway," he explained.

"Why now?" Jessie asked.

James shook his head. "I don't know." He hesitated. "Because I don't want any secrets between us anymore. Because I think you should read what she had to say to me. Because I miss you and want to come home."

Jessie steadied herself against the grocery cart. "Read it to me," she said, surprising both of them. "You read it to me."

James stood watching his wife, the letter still in his hand, extended to her. He glanced around them, the busy parking lot, people and cars coming and going. He nodded. He opened the letter and read:

Dear James,

I know that we have enjoyed something special between us. I know that we have had good times together. Lisa loves you like a father. And

I will always thank you for your kindnesses toward her and toward me.

I am asking that you don't come back to the apartment and that you don't call or contact me. We need to end our relationship. It isn't because I don't have feelings for you. Quite the opposite, in fact, I have many deep feelings for you. I love you. But that can't change what you have in your heart. You are still bound to your wife and you clearly struggle with the decision that you made to leave her and your family. And somehow, as much as I thought I could respect that decision you made, I can't because it was a wrong decision. And you know it. And until you deal with your choices and make right what has been wrong, you will never be fully available to anyone. I do not wish to participate in letting you deny what is in your heart. I do not wish to be involved with a man pretending that he has made things right in his life. I cannot be a crutch or a substitute. I deserve more than that and I deserve to be with a person who is completely committed to our relationship and not just looking for a reason not to deal with his past. I also would never be able to respect in fullness anyone who ran away from a marriage and a family. To choose not to say good-bye, not to explain why you left, not to go and face the consequences of your behavior are the choices of a man I can't respect. And respect is the key to trust and trust is necessary for love.

Go home, James Jenkins, even if it's to say good-bye. Go home and face your wife and tell her what is in your heart. Either you love her or you don't, but every person deserves to hear the truth, and every person ought to bear that responsibility. You're a good man, James, and I don't understand why you're here. I am a better person for having known you, and you are better than this choice that you made. Find your way and go home.

In hopes for your peace,

Ramona

James folded up the letter and placed it back in the envelope. He looked up at his wife, trying to measure her reaction to what he had read. There was a long pause.

She shook her head and glanced across the parking lot. "I miss Margaret," she said, and dabbed at her eyes.

There was a pause. A breeze stirred, and a few old leaves danced around their feet.

"I miss her too, Jess," James said. He leaned down to pick up a plastic bag that had landed near them. "I have thought about what she would tell us, what she'd say to me after what happened to us. I've wondered if she would hate me too."

Jessie placed the tissue back in her purse. "She wouldn't hate you, James. I don't hate you." She smoothed down the front of her jacket. "Margaret would say I was being too hard on you. That's what she'd tell us."

James studied his wife's face and waited to see if she would explain what she meant. He stuck the plastic bag down inside one of his bags.

"I already know what she would say because I've asked her a hundred times in these last six weeks and she always says the same thing." Jessie shook her head and drew in a breath.

"She would tell me that what happened between you and that woman happened a long time ago, and that the biggest hurdle we had we have already overcome, and that was the one when you came to Hope Springs for Wallace and Lana's wedding and me making the decision of whether or not to take you back. She would tell me that we spent enough time apart and that life is short and that we love each other and that I should quit being so hard on you, that I should quit punishing you because in the end you chose me, you chose to come home, and I now have the choice of love or bitterness." Jessie cleared her throat, her voice straining a bit. "And she would say, 'Jessie Jenkins, when have you ever chosen anything other than love?' that's what Margaret Peele would say." She tugged at the bottom of her jacket and looked directly at her husband.

James waited. He looked away and wiped his eyes. And then, he nodded. "You're absolutely right. That's exactly what Margaret would say."

Jessie stood up tall. She lifted her chin. "You didn't have to show me the letter. It wouldn't have mattered to Margaret what that woman had to say and it shouldn't have mattered to me." She paused. "You should come home," she said to her husband. "Throw the letter away and come home." And she reached out and he wept, taking his wife by the hand.

Chopped Chipped Beef Dip

8 ounces cream cheese, softened
½ cup sour cream
⅓ cup chopped green pepper
2 tablespoons chopped onion
dash garlic salt
½ teaspoon salt
3 ounces chipped beef, finely chopped
1 cup chopped pecans
1 tablespoon butter

Mix all ingredients except pecans and butter. Place in 9-inch baking dish. Sauté pecans in butter and cover mixture with nuts. Bake at 350 degrees for 20 minutes. Great with crackers.

—Beatrice Witherspoon

Chapter Nineteen

Robin was the last person Beatrice expected to find standing on her doorstep when the doorbell rang. Beatrice thought it was Eldon dropping off her mail or the copy store bringing her the box of finished wedding cookbooks for Jessie and James that she had been told would be delivered sometime that day. She opened the door and stood staring at her daughter in utter shock.

"Hello, Mom," the young woman said.

Beatrice still could not respond. In all her fantasies of what she would say to Robin when they did finally see each other, she had been smart and witty and always knew the right way to begin the conversation. Once she was faced with the reality of standing inches away from her daughter, she couldn't think of a word to say.

"Can I come in?" Robin asked.

Bea tried to shake off the shock. "Of course, of course," she finally answered, and moved aside so that her daughter could walk in. Robin had a small bouquet of flowers in her hands and as she walked past Beatrice, she handed them to her mother. "I bought these for you. I know how you love peonies."

"Yes, thank you," Bea responded, taking the flowers and sounding like a robot. "I'll, um, get them in a vase." And she hurried off to the kitchen, leaving Robin standing by the front door. Suddenly she remembered what she had done and she hurried back into the foyer. "Oh, please," she said. "Come in, I'm sorry."

Robin followed her mother into the kitchen. Beatrice reached into a cabinet and pulled out a vase. She placed the flowers in it and filled the vase with water. She set them by the sink. "They're quite lovely," she commented. "I can't seem to get peonies to grow here." She looked up at her daughter. "Please sit down," and she motioned toward a chair at the kitchen table. "You want something to drink?" she asked, and made her way to the refrigerator.

Robin shook her head. "No, I just had some iced tea."

"Oh," Bea responded. "You've been in town awhile?" she asked, still in her polite tone of voice. She glanced over at the clock, seeing that it was eleven. She wondered if Robin had been in town all morning. She wondered how long she was going to stay.

"I just drove in," Robin explained. "But I stopped in Lexington for a glass of tea," she added, referring to a town near Hope Springs. "Bojangles'," she explained. "You know how I love their iced tea."

"Yes, I remember," Bea said, taking a seat across from her daughter, recalling how they used to stop at one of the fast food chains every Sunday after church when Robin was young. "Gravy biscuits and sweet tea," she added, naming the meal that they used to enjoy.

"Nothing's changed, except I don't do gravy biscuits so much anymore." Robin rubbed her belly. "Now that I'm middle-aged, I've got to watch those calories, you know."

Bea smiled.

The two women sat awkwardly for a few minutes. Then they both spoke at the same time. Beatrice was asking her about her job and Robin was commenting on the flowers growing in her mother's front yard. They both stopped and looked at each other.

"You go," Robin instructed.

Bea shook her head. "I was just asking about your job."

"Oh, it's fine. Still bank work, you know." She nodded and placed her hands on the table. "A little harder since the recession, but I'm still happy there. Plus I'm really glad to have a job."

Beatrice glanced down and suddenly noticed the engagement ring on Robin's finger. She reached over and took her daughter's hand. She studied it a few minutes before commenting. "It's a beauty," she finally said.

"Farrell picked it out," Robin explained, smiling.

Beatrice got up from the table. "I think I'll have some lemonade. You sure you don't want any?"

She pulled out two glasses and looked back at her daughter.

Robin shook her head.

Beatrice put one of the glasses up and filled the other with ice, then pulled a pitcher out of the refrigerator and poured herself a glass. She moved back over to the table and sat down again.

"How's Dick?" Robin asked about her stepfather, sounding uncomfortable trying to make small talk.

"Good," Beatrice replied. "I thought you two had spoken recently," she added, recalling that Dick had made the wedding RSVP call and handled all the arrangements for the two of them.

"You're right," Robin answered. "We have."

Beatrice nodded, taking a sip of her drink.

Robin took in a deep breath. "I'm sorry," she confessed. "I know I should have told you when I got engaged and when we made plans for the wedding. I'm sorry." She looked down at her hands still clasped in front of her.

"When you got engaged?" Bea responded. "That's the first time you think I'd want to know what was going on in your life? Why wouldn't you have told me when you fell in love? When you knew he was the one you thought you might want to marry?"

Robin glanced up and looked at her mother. "I was just never sure when that happened," she replied.

"You didn't know when this guy became special for you?" Bea asked.

Robin shrugged. "I knew I had feelings for him. I've had a crush on him for years but he was never really . . . I don't know." She hesitated. "Interested in me," she finished her thought.

"Is he somebody from work?" Bea asked, trying to learn as much as she could about her future son-in-law. She wasn't letting on but somehow she was starting to feel as if something wasn't quite right about this engagement and upcoming wedding.

Robin shook her head. "He goes to the same gym I go to," she replied.

Beatrice nodded. "So, you've had a crush on him and you waited around for years and he finally noticed you?"

Robin smiled. "I guess that's about right," she answered.

"And when was that?" Bea asked.

"When was what?" Robin responded, unclear of what her mother wanted to know.

"When did he finally notice you?" she explained her question.

"Oh, um . . ." She thought for a moment. "We've been dating about fourteen months," she replied.

Bea just kept nodding her head as if she was suddenly beginning to understand something she hadn't been able to before.

"And in these fourteen months, you only thought about telling me about him, about the two of you, when you became engaged?" The hurt was obvious in her voice.

"Everything just kept moving faster and faster and I kept thinking, I need to let Mom know, and then before I knew it, we were booking an outdoor garden for the wedding in Cabo."

"You came home for the holidays," Bea recounted. "That was during those fourteen months. That would have meant you were dating him then." She leaned in toward her daughter. "You never mentioned him. You never mentioned anything about him."

Robin's face reddened. "It was complicated at first," she noted.

"What does that mean?" Bea asked.

Robin shook her head as if she didn't want to explain.

"Complicated because of me?" Beatrice was trying to understand.

"No," Robin answered.

"Complicated because of what? You didn't want him to meet your family? He didn't want to meet us? Because—" She stopped, suddenly beginning to figure out what Robin was not saying. "Because he was married?" she asked.

Robin looked up. Hearing her mother's question surprised her. And it was obvious that Beatrice had stumbled upon the right answer. "Robin, he was married when you were dating?" she asked. "You had an affair and now you're marrying him?" She stood up from the table and then sat back down. "Oh me," she said, wringing her hands. "Don't you know this never works?" she asked.

"And that is why I haven't said anything. I knew you'd judge me and not give us a chance." Robin folded her arms across her chest and slumped in her chair.

"No, that is not the reason you didn't say anything. The reason is because you knew what you were doing was wrong and you knew I would know it." Bea kept shaking her head. "How long has he been divorced?" she asked.

"It's been final for two months," was the answer. "But he was separated when we met. He had already moved out. I didn't break up a marriage," she added.

"How do you know he had really moved out?" Beatrice was recalling the numerous stories she had heard from friends and acquaintances about people having affairs and swearing to their lovers that they were separated. She thought of the thousands of movies that included that as part of the plotline. She almost brought up one but then thought better of it.

"He told me and I believe him."

"He told you at the gym, when he finally noticed you, that he was separated and was planning to be divorced?" Bea was trying to make sense of the situation as well as trying to get her daughter to hear how unlikely this story was.

Robin shrugged. "Something like that," she answered softly.

Beatrice gave out a long sigh and shook her head as if she was disappointed.

"What happened to his first marriage?"

Robin rolled her eyes as if she didn't want to continue with this line of questioning, but she answered. "They just fell out of love."

"Does he have children?" Bea asked.

"Two," Robin replied. "And they're great. They like me and I really like them. One's a boy, he's eleven, and the little girl is six."

Beatrice stood up again and then sat back down. She took a sip of her drink. "How do you know the same thing won't happen to this marriage? How do you know he has worked through all of the trouble, made closure? How do you know that in a couple of years he won't notice someone else and tell her that he's separated from his second wife?" She stamped her foot a number of times. "Robin, you've never been in love, how do you know he really loves you?" And as soon as she asked the question, she could feel how it stung.

Robin raised her eyebrows and then began pulling at strands of her hair, something Beatrice remembered as a nervous habit Robin had since she was a little girl.

She reached over for Robin's hand. "I'm sorry. That wasn't a fair question. Of course he loves you," Bea said. "He's marrying you, of course he loves you," she repeated.

Robin dropped her eyes away from her mother. She stopped pulling her hair and rested her hands in her lap, not taking her mother's hand that remained stretched before her.

"Robin, you have never thought you were good enough for anybody. You have always compared yourself to your sister and measured yourself, every time coming out on the losing end. All I have ever wanted for you is to find somebody who really loves you, who knows how incredible you are." Bea pulled her hands back and placed her arms down by her sides. She tried to make herself believe what she was about to say. She took in a breath. "I'm happy you've found Farrell. It sounds like you have been attracted to him for a long time. I'm sure that this timing is right and that this marriage will bring you both much happiness."

"I really think you'll like him," Robin said, appearing to cheer up a bit. "He's kind of like Daddy was," she added.

Beatrice smiled, thinking about her first husband, Paul. They had been in love at one time, and even though what had been lovely in the beginning didn't last and even though the relationship wasn't as deep and wonderful in the end before he died, she had loved her husband. They had managed to have a good marriage. He had been faithful and supportive. In his own way, she knew that he had loved her.

Still, Beatrice was glad she had found Dick. He had been as much a true friend as he had been a husband. And he had made her feel alive in a way she hadn't in a long time. He made her laugh and notice things she usually hurried past. He treated her as if she was the most important person alive. Beatrice knew that she was lucky to have had a second chance at love. And when that thought entered her mind, she suddenly realized that she ought to offer the same hope to this young man who was to be her son-in-law.

Marriages break up all the time, she thought. It was a sad fact, but true. So, if Farrell Monk's marriage ended and he met Robin near the time that it happened or was going to happen, who was she to judge? It certainly sounded as if her daughter had loved him from a distance for a long time. Besides, Bea told herself as she sat watching her daughter, she had been a parent long enough to know she was not going to be able to save her children from trouble. As much as she wished she had the power to do that, Beatrice had learned, everybody has to walk his own path. And, she thought, the love that we find and keep, the love that we have taken from us, the love we pretend is there and isn't, and the love that surprises us, all of that cannot be managed and handled by anyone's mother. That, Beatrice understood, is a part of those paths we claim as our own, and nobody can save us or keep us from what happens in love.

She smiled at her daughter, hopeful and radiant with a mother's affection, and reached out her hands to her daughter again. This time Robin took them.

"So, what can I help you do to get ready for your big day?" she asked, and it was as if a huge burden had been hoisted from her shoulders. "Would you like a special cookbook for the occasion?"

And Robin simply laughed.

Darlene's Mini Sandwiches

8 ounces cream cheese, softened
½ cup finely chopped walnuts
4 ounces drained crushed pineapple
dash hot pepper sauce
1½ to 2 loaves wheat bread

Mix first four ingredients until smooth. Refrigerate overnight. Take out a couple of hours before making sandwiches. Cut crusts off bread. Spread to desired thickness on bread. Cut sandwiches in sixths. Makes about 9 dozen.

—Darlene K.

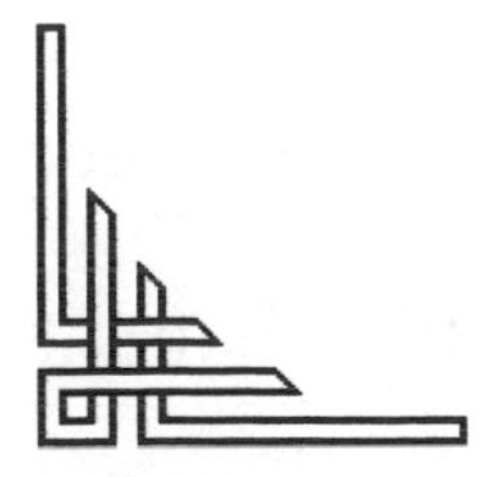

Chapter Twenty

When Charlotte found out from Darlene that Christine, the newest resident, the pregnant one, had left sometime in the middle of the night, returning to her violent husband just released from jail, she sat down at her desk and cried. It wasn't like her to take that kind of news so hard; after all, it happened a lot. But for some reason, this time, this girl and her unborn baby, walking back into such an explosive and violent situation, pushed her over the edge.

Charlotte wasn't naïve. She knew she couldn't save all the women. She knew some of the women, no, most of the women, couldn't imagine their lives without the men who beat them. She knew that one in four women was a victim of domestic abuse, and most of those victims could never find a way to get out. And even when they did, even when they found St. Mary's, found a support system, found other women who encouraged them, found out there was another way of life, even then a lot of them ended right back in the hold of the very men who brutalized them.

"Did anybody try to stop her?" Charlotte asked, wiping her face.

Darlene shook her head. "We didn't know until

we heard the front door shut," she replied. She stood at the office door.

"I thought she had made up her mind to leave him," Charlotte said, pulling another tissue from the box. "I thought she was moving back to Albuquerque with her grandmother."

"That's what she told us too," Darlene said. "I don't know when she talked to him or how he found her, but somehow they must have communicated," she added. She wrapped her arms around herself. "How did he get out of jail?" she asked.

"Somebody posted his bail a couple of days ago and she never did press charges," Charlotte replied. "She lied to me about that. And lucky for him, he pays for a good lawyer."

"Rich men," Darlene noted. "They're the worst ones. They always find a way out of everything. They always develop some defense, make up some excuse, or have some secret relationship with a judge. At least with the poor ones they have to cool off in a cell a few weeks before they get back to the streets."

Charlotte was still visibly shaken. "I just don't understand why she went back to him. He broke her nose. He whipped her with a belt." She threw the used tissue away and pulled out another.

"It's hard when you're pregnant." Darlene moved inside the office and sat down in the chair across from Charlotte. "It's harder to leave," she added.

Charlotte looked up. "Why would it be harder then? I don't understand. Doesn't a woman realize that when she's pregnant that staying in a violent situation is even more dangerous, and for a baby, a child, not just her?"

Darlene shrugged. "It just doesn't work like that," she replied. "A woman thinks being pregnant will make the difference. She thinks that if her man knows he has a baby, that she's carrying his baby, that it will be the one thing that stops him from hitting her."

"Christine is seven months pregnant. He whipped her like a dog. He made her get stitches. And she's seven months pregnant!" Charlotte yelled. "Why would she think he's going to stop when she's eight months pregnant or when that baby is due?" She dropped her head in her hands. "Jesus, for the life of me, Darlene, this doesn't make sense!"

Darlene didn't respond. The two women sat in the office for a few minutes without further conversation. None of the other residents were around. Only Iris was still close, and she was in the back taking a shower. The house was quiet.

"He beat her when they were dating for three years and she married him anyway," Charlotte said. "And now he beats her when she's pregnant. You're telling me that she really thinks having a baby will change him?"

"I'm telling you that it's just hard, complicated.

A woman like Christine, she's locked up in her mind. It's hard to do different after you've lived your whole life in that kind of thinking." Darlene shook her head. "It's hard to change when you only know one way. And she only knows one way. She only knows violence. Look, Christine at least now knows that you're here, and that's important. She knows there's a place where she can get to."

"And so does he." Charlotte wiped her eyes again and then rubbed her forehead with her fingers. "Carla said she saw the lights in the driveway at two this morning. That means somebody picked her up. That was probably him, don't you think?"

Darlene glanced down at the floor. She knew how dangerous it was when the perpetrators knew the address of the shelter.

"St. Mary's has been here too long. We need another place. We need a gate and security. We need another place," Charlotte repeated, dropping back in her chair.

"He won't remember where he picked her up." Darlene tried to sound convincing. She knew, however, just like Charlotte, that these men, these violent spouses and boyfriends, would do anything, kill or hurt anybody, if they thought someone was hiding their women. When she had moved into the shelter months before there was a security guard, but due to budget cuts, they had to let him go. “He’s got what he wanted,” she added, trying to remain upbeat and positive. “He has no reason to come back.”

Charlotte closed her eyes and massaged her temples. “I need to call the police to let them know,” she said with a sigh. “There’s likely to be another 911 call from the home address in the next few weeks.”

She opened a drawer and pulled out a page of names and contacts. She picked up the phone and dialed a number. “I swear, doing this work really makes a woman want to stay single,” she said to Darlene as she waited for an answer on the other end of the line.

She made the report, explaining the details to the officer on duty. When she hung up the phone, Darlene was still sitting across from her and appeared as if she wanted to talk about something.

“So, tell me about your date with Officer Love.” She knew that Charlotte had gone out the previous night because Carla had announced it to the women at dinner. Charlotte never told anyone when she had a date, but since Carla had moved into the shelter, the women always seemed to know.

“We had a fight,” Charlotte responded. Though she usually was not one to share details of her private life, she and Darlene had become friends over the months that Darlene had been a resident at St. Mary’s. Besides, after Christine had left in the middle of the night and after such a horrible night with Donovan, she needed to talk to someone.

"Oh," Darlene said, sounding surprised. "About what?" she asked.

"My work, this place." She rolled her eyes.

"Carla?" Darlene added.

Charlotte glanced up. She was glad to have Darlene as a friend, but she suddenly realized the implications of the conversation. She knew better than to talk about one resident at the shelter with another. She didn't answer.

"It's okay. You don't have to say but it's pretty obvious," Darlene noted. "Carla and Donovan are way too chummy for exes."

"You want a cup of coffee?" Charlotte asked, hoping for that line of questioning to end.

Darlene shook her head. "You tell him how you feel?" she asked, not following suit with Charlotte. "Is that why you fought?"

Charlotte got up from her seat and went over to the coffeepot on the small table in the corner of her office. She poured a cup and sat back down. "It's really not a good thing for us to be discussing," she pointed out.

"It's all right, I'm not saying anything to anybody," Darlene said. "Does he know how awkward this is for you?" she asked.

Charlotte hesitated before answering. She was tired. She had not slept much since the argument. "He feels responsible for her," she finally replied.

"Of course he does," Darlene noted. "He's her first love, her ex-husband, a police officer, and a Navajo. That's a lot of ties that bind," she added.

Charlotte smiled. "All true."

Darlene studied Charlotte. "That doesn't mean he loves her or wants to be back with her."

Charlotte shrugged, took a sip. "Honestly, I really shouldn't be talking to you about this. It's not professional for the executive director to be discussing one resident with another resident."

"I'm no longer a resident, remember? Today's my moving day," Darlene noted.

Charlotte glanced up at Darlene and nodded. She had helped Darlene find an apartment in town. Darlene was enrolled in nursing classes at the community college and had been clean and sober for ten months. She had changed her last name and was starting her new life in a matter of hours. The two of them were planning to go shopping first thing that morning to purchase items for the new place. The shopping trip had been postponed, however, because of the early morning departure of the new resident. Charlotte cleared her throat. "And this should be a day of celebration, not a day of mourning or commiseration."

"It's a day," Darlene responded. "And most days have celebrations and commiserations," she added.

Charlotte smiled. "True," she said.

"So, answer me, have you told Donovan how you feel?" Darlene asked again.

Charlotte looked at Darlene, trying to decide if she was going to talk about this with her or not. "He knows that I'm uncomfortable with the relationship," she replied.

Darlene nodded. "And he just thinks you're being jealous?" she asked.

"I don't know exactly what he thinks," Charlotte answered. "I got a feeling that the two of them are up to something, but he won't tell me what it is. He denies that there's anything between them."

"You mean like the two of them are planning some revenge?" Darlene asked.

Charlotte studied Darlene, trying to see if she had heard something.

"I'm just guessing," Darlene explained. "Carla's not mentioned anything to me," she added, understanding what the look on Charlotte's face meant.

"I don't know. I've just got a funny feeling about things," Charlotte said. "They just seem to have something important they talk about together, a lot."

"And you asked him about it?" Darlene was curious.

"He said that they were just trying to figure out where she could go and what she can do to stay away from her husband."

There was a pause.

"Carla has a place to go," Darlene said.

Charlotte shook her head. "Her sister said no. Her mother doesn't have room. We talked about that."

Darlene waited. "That's not true," she said. "Her sister said yes." She hesitated. "Carla said no," she explained.

Charlotte looked surprised but then she shrugged. "It doesn't matter," she responded. "She gets to choose where she wants to go. She leaves when she finds suitable housing, a safe and comfortable living situation," she added.

"Her sister has a three-bedroom house in Farmington. She can get Carla a job at the restaurant she manages. She wants Carla to live with her because she needs help with the mortgage and her little boy."

This was news Charlotte hadn't heard. She had been told that Carla's sister had a studio apartment and that they didn't get along and that her sister was unemployed and a deadbeat. Carla had told her that she had no possible housing opportunities with any family members.

"She's staying here because of Donovan," Darlene explained.

Charlotte shook her head. "You shouldn't be telling me this," she said. "I shouldn't be talking to you about this," she added.

Darlene shrugged. "I just thought you should know. Carla talks way too much and she said that she didn't want to leave Gallup just yet. She said she's working things out with Donovan."

"What does that mean?" Charlotte asked, now interested in what Darlene had to say.

Darlene shrugged. "I don't know. It could be what you're thinking, something about revenge." She stopped. "Or it could be their relationship. I get the feeling she isn't over her first husband."

The two women looked at each other.

"Well, I can't do anything about Carla and Donovan. They need to figure things out for themselves. If they want to get back together, then they will. If they're planning some act of vengeance against her husband, I can't stop that either. Nothing I can say will change things." Charlotte drank her coffee and set her cup on the desk.

"You can tell Carla to go live with her sister," Darlene said.

"Because I want her away from Donovan? Because I don't trust her alone with my boyfriend?" Charlotte asked. "I'm not that underhanded," she said. "I just don't work that way."

Darlene stretched her legs in front of her and lifted her arms high above her head, clasped her fingers together, and then dropped them behind her head. "I'm just saying, Carla isn't telling you the truth about her sister and that living arrangement. And she's better now and her husband is locked up. If she was anybody else, wouldn't you have urged her to move on?"

Charlotte thought about the question. She shook her head again. "I think I am not meant to be involved with Donovan, or with any other man, for that matter." She stood up from her chair and sorted a few papers together, stuck them in a folder, and placed them in a box at the corner of the desk. “I know too much,” she added. “I’m not sure I can ever fully trust a man after all I’ve seen here.”

Darlene leaned forward in her chair. “That doesn’t sound like the optimistic, hopeful shelter executive director I know. Weren’t you the one who told me I could beat my addictions to drugs and to violent men? Weren’t you the woman who said I was the only one who could decide what I wanted with my life and then go and get it? And yes, if I remember correctly, weren’t you the one who said there is enough good love out there in the world that I didn’t ever have to settle for bad love or being alone again?”

Charlotte studied the woman sitting before her. She had, indeed, been the one to say all those things to the resident at the shelter. She had always been the one filled with hope for the women at St. Mary’s. She had always believed that life could be different for all of them if they really wanted to change. She looked away and put the contact list back in the drawer beside her.

“We are getting ready to get you on your way to a brand-new life. You have done amazing work, and things for you are going to be different.” She picked up her purse and grabbed her car keys. “But Darlene, I’ve learned that some things don’t change.” She walked around the desk. “Maybe I’m just not meant to be in love. Maybe I'm one of those women like Christine and I'm just stuck in my thinking. And right now I'm thinking it's not so bad being alone."

Darlene didn't respond. She stood up.

"So, let's go get you some towels and a mop. You have a new life to start!" And Charlotte smiled and headed out the door while Darlene stood waiting. Finally she followed Charlotte, and the two of them left St. Mary's.

Maria's Wedding Puffs

1¼ cups small-curd cottage cheese
2¼ cups sharp cheddar cheese, shredded
1 small onion, minced
¼ teaspoon salt
½ cup chopped green chiles
2 eggs
¾ cup water
¾ cup flour
pepper to taste

Mix first five ingredients until well blended. Chill the mix until firm. Beat together eggs, water, and pepper. Add flour and blend thoroughly. Chill this batter until thick. Form the cheese mixture into small balls. Then dip them in the batter, making sure that they are completely covered. Fry them in 3 inches of hot oil until golden. Drain and serve immediately.

—Maria Roybal

Chapter Twenty-one

"Well, what happened to the two of them?" Beatrice had called St. Mary's after spending only a few hours with Charlotte, who had just come back to Hope Springs. She knew there had been a split but she had been unable to get any details from Charlotte. All Charlotte had said was that she and Donovan just decided to quit seeing each other. "Did he break up with her because she can't cook, because she's a minister?"

"Isn't she there?" Maria asked. She was very uncomfortable talking about this subject with Beatrice. She knew that Charlotte had flown back to North Carolina for her friend's wedding renewal service. She glanced at the clock and knew that Charlotte should have been back in her hometown for a number of hours. Maria and Gilbert had taken her to Albuquerque to the airport. "Can't you ask her these questions?"

"Well, of course she's here, Maria," Beatrice huffed into the phone. "You know that. How else would I have known they broke up? And of course I have asked her these questions," she added. "She's just not talking."

"Ah," Maria responded. *"Charlotte, es la más cuidadita."*

"Yes, she is the silent one but I need to know

details," Beatrice explained. "What happened between her and the policeman?"

"Sister Charlotte should tell you herself," Maria noted, trying to sound professional. She didn't want to get in trouble again for telling too much information to Charlotte's friends in North Carolina.

"Maria Roybal, you know that Charlotte isn't going to tell us anything. So fill me in, what happened with her and her officer? Was he taking money from the bad guys? Was he running some scam that she found out about?"

Maria sighed into the phone. *"Señor, perdóname,"* she said, and made the sign of the cross on her chest.

"Is it the ex-wife? It's her, isn't it? What, did she cause trouble again? Did they become involved?" She paused. "Wait a minute. Wasn't she supposed to move out on her own last month?"

"I cannot talk about the ex-wife," Maria answered. She waited.

"Okay, what can you talk about?" Beatrice understood Maria wouldn't talk about Carla.

"I can talk about a stubborn woman who would rather live her life as a lonely old maid than try to make things work with a responsible, loving man."

"Charlotte?" Bea responded. "She did this?" she asked. "She broke up with him?"

"Sí," Maria answered.

"But why?" Beatrice asked.

"She is stubborn, I say."

"But had something happened?" Beatrice wanted to know. "Was she still upset about his first marriage?" She hesitated and then added, "That first marriage that I know you can't talk about. Didn't she think they were doing something together in secret? Did she catch him in a lie?"

"You still watching dirty television movies?" Maria asked.

"No, I am not watching dirty television movies," Beatrice replied.

There was a pause.

"You get arrested for stealing the cable?" Maria asked. She had heard from Charlotte about Beatrice's television arrangement. The two of them had laughed about it.

"No, I did not get arrested," Beatrice responded. There was a pause. "I just got the bill is all," she added.

"How much was the bill?" Maria asked.

Beatrice cleared her throat. "We are not talking about my utilities at the moment. I want to know what happened with Charlotte and her beau. Did she catch him cheating on her?"

"She didn't catch him in anything." Maria answered. "He tried to explain how he and *you know who* were just trying to find her a condo in Arizona and that he didn't love her, just wanted to protect her. But Sister Charlotte would have none of it, said that they could never make it work because of their too many differences."

"She said that?" Beatrice asked, sounding very surprised. "Charlotte loves their differences. She made that very clear when she told me about him. Why would she say that?"

"I don't know for sure," Maria replied. "But I have my thoughts," she added.

"Well, let's hear them," Beatrice responded.

Maria waited, trying to decide if she should talk to Beatrice about her ideas. She knew Gilbert was tired of hearing them. She looked around to see if anyone else was listening to her conversation. No one was at the shelter. She forged ahead. "All she sees here is bad marriages that end in violence. All she sees is controlling husbands. She thinks she would end up like these girls."

"But the policeman wouldn't beat her." Beatrice paused. "Would he?" She gasped. "He didn't hit her, did he?" she shouted.

"No, no, no," Maria yelled into the receiver. "Officer Sanchez would never raise his hand. It's her. It's Charlotte. She just doesn't want to get hurt and all she sees is women who get hurt." Maria made a clucking noise. "I try to get her to come to church, to the couples' class with women her age, come to book club, see other people happy and in love, but she spends all her time here. But then, maybe I helped this happen. I said too much to her about Officer Sanchez. I should have minded my own business."

Beatrice thought about what Maria was saying. "When did this happen?" she asked.

Maria hesitated. "Three weeks ago," she replied.

"Three weeks?" Beatrice asked, sounding surprised. "And she never said anything to me all these times we've talked in three weeks?" Beatrice recalled they had spoken a number of times to discuss the renewal ceremony and Charlotte's travel itinerary. She was shocked to know that in all those conversations Charlotte had not mentioned the breakup.

"She didn't tell me until last weekend. I asked her if she was bringing Donovan to a party in town, it's a carnival at my church for children, and Charlotte always goes and takes the children from the shelter. It's a lot of fun, with nice foods like those puffs I told you about, one of those big blow-up bouncy houses with all those balloons and balls inside, and face painting and—"

"I get it, Maria, a carnival, I get it," Beatrice interrupted. "And that was when she said they broke up?"

"Sí," Maria answered. "She came to the carnival without him," she added. "He was there and she would not speak to him."

"But why would she break up with him now? I really thought she cared for this man."

"She is afraid, Bea. He was starting to get very serious with Sister Charlotte. He was here all the time. He was giving her flowers, taking her home to meet his family. I was starting really to like him too. And since, well, *you know who* has been gone . . ."

"Carla," Beatrice noted, saying her name because she knew Maria wouldn't.

"Since she has been gone, I thought the two of them were deep in love. I thought he might propose," Maria added.

"Really? Propose?" Beatrice asked, sounding very surprised. "It was that serious between them?"

"Sí," Maria answered. "That serious, yes. He was here every day, and then, I don't know. Something just happened."

There was a pause.

"She snapped," Beatrice said.

"Snap?" Maria said in reply, sounding confused. "What is snap?"

"Snapped," Beatrice corrected her. "You know, her nerves broke, she arrived at a point of no return."

"You see this before?" Maria asked.

"Lots of times," Beatrice answered, sounding very smug.

"On your television movies?" Maria asked.

"And in real life," Beatrice replied.

"You see Sister Charlotte snap?" Maria wanted to know.

"Well, no, not Charlotte. I've just seen it happen to women when they think they're getting ready to be asked to make a commitment." She paused. "Although, now that I think about it, it's usually men."

"Who snap?" Maria asked, intrigued by Beatrice's line of thinking.

"Yes, who snap," Beatrice answered.

The two women waited. They were both considering the notion that Charlotte might have lost her nerve.

"So, Jessie and James get all their stuff fixed?" Maria asked, changing the subject and recalling why Charlotte had returned to North Carolina. She knew about everything that had been going on in Hope Springs because she and Beatrice talked quite often.

"Seems so," Beatrice replied. "They were meant to be together. Even though they were apart for such a long time, they're just like any old married couple," she added.

"And are you still going to your daughter's wedding next week?" Maria asked. She also knew that Beatrice had mentioned the possibility of missing the destination wedding, and in all their conversations, she hadn't been updated about Robin's visit.

"Dick and I made arrangements to go," Beatrice replied. "Robin and I worked things out," she added.

"Ah, God is good," Maria announced. "You and

your daughter needed to talk. I'm glad that happened, Bea."

"Yes, well, what are you going to do, right?" Bea asked. She sighed.

"What's wrong?" Maria asked.

"I just don't think it's going to work out between them," she replied. "He's got children and an ex-wife, and I don't know, I just don't think he's been honest with Robin," she added. "It all happened too fast."

"Did you tell her about your concerns?" Maria asked.

"I tried, but it took her so long just to tell me about the wedding, I decided not to say anything." Beatrice paused. "I was trying not to meddle," she added.

"El dolor de las madres," Maria said, and then translated into English, "The burden of mothers."

"You can say that again," Beatrice responded. "I figure they'll manage things together and she'll find out sooner or later about this guy."

Maria made a kind of humming noise. "And your friend Louise," she asked. "Is her husband dead?"

"Died last week," Beatrice answered. "She should be back in Hope Springs for the renewal service this weekend too."

"You have missed her, yes?" Maria asked.

"Yes, I have missed her," Beatrice replied.

The two women paused.

"And I have missed Charlotte," Beatrice added. "And I'm concerned about her."

"Yes, so am I," Maria noted. "But what is there to do?" she asked.

There was another long pause.

"Perhaps we can figure out something to do," Beatrice said.

"What are you thinking, Bea?" Maria could tell that she was plotting something.

"I'm not sure," Beatrice replied. "But I will need Officer Tall, Dark, and Handsome's phone number," she said.

"Oh no," Maria responded. "Sister Charlotte would kill me if she knew I gave you Donovan's number. She would kill me if she knew we were talking about the two of them and that I told you what I know."

"What have you told me?" Beatrice asked, trying to sound coy. "All you've said is that they didn't go to the church carnival together and that you're worried about her. She told me they broke up, and even though I called, you don't know any of the details either."

"I cannot give you his telephone number," Maria stated.

"Maria, come on, I can just get my neighbor's ten-year-old to find it on the computer if I have to. Or I can call the Gallup police station and ask." She paused. "Oh, just give me the number. You know I'm going to find it whether you give it to me or not. And you know that somebody needs to step in and do something about this." She waited. "Maria, who are we if we are not the good friends who keep the flame of love burning?"

Maria made the sign of the cross over herself again. And then she pulled out the phone book and found the number. She read it out and then said, "You must never tell her that I was involved." She mumbled something in Spanish and closed the phone book. "If Sister Charlotte knows that I was the one who helped you in this, she will fire me and Gilbert will divorce me."

"Charlotte will not know that I called you and she can't fire you, you're a volunteer." Bea paused as she finished jotting down the number. "And Gilbert will not divorce you because he knows what a lucky man he is." She waited and then knew what Maria was doing because Charlotte had told her about the volunteer's habit of crossing herself when she was nervous. "And stop crossing yourself. God likes it when we step in on love's behalf. I know because I saw it in a movie."

And Maria shook her head and rolled her eyes while she heard the phone on the other end hang up.

Margaret's Cheese Straws

1 pound sharp cheddar cheese, shredded
2 cups flour
¼ teaspoon cayenne pepper (or less if desired)
1 stick margarine
1 teaspoon salt

Mix all ingredients well and roll out. Cut into small strips like straws. Bake at 425 degrees until golden brown.

—From Margaret Peele's recipes

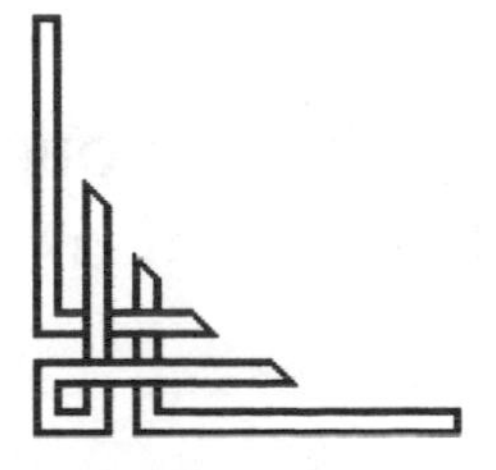

Chapter Twenty-two

"Well, fancy meeting you all here!" Louise was passing the cemetery on her way into town when she saw the familiar cars and turned around. She yelled at the women as she was walking toward them.

Jessie, Beatrice, and Charlotte had gone to Margaret's grave the evening before the ceremony to place flowers and to pay their respects together. They had placed a blanket on the grave and were sitting together enjoying glasses of champagne.

"Preacher Charlotte!" Louise exclaimed as she saw her friend and walked over to her. "What a sight for old eyes you are!"

"Sweet Louise," Charlotte stood up and said with a grin. "I was hoping you'd make it here before the ceremony." They hugged tightly as the other women stood.

"Well, something looks different about you," Beatrice noted, stepping over to greet her friend. "But it's certainly not because you look like the blushing bride."

"I guess that's what happens after a certain age." Louise smiled and hugged Beatrice.

"Louise, my love, it is sure good to have you home." Jessie moved over to greet her friend as well.

"And speaking of blushing brides, you look beautiful," Louise said, holding out her hands and taking a long look at Jessie, who had just had her hair and nails done. She was glowing.

"It all seems so silly," Jessie replied, dropping her arms.

"Nothing silly about it," Louise responded. "I think it's high time that man gave you a real wedding complete with a fine shindig."

"You seemed to have done fine without all of the hullabaloo," Beatrice said.

"Ah, Bea, you still mad I didn't let you plan a wedding ceremony for me and George?" Louise asked. "That you didn't get to put together some nice recipes?"

Beatrice shook her head. "I thought our little get-together at Lester's was quite lovely," she replied.

"Indeed, it was," Louise noted. "So, Charlotte, when did you arrive in Hope Springs?" she asked. She walked over and took Charlotte by the hands.

"Yesterday," she replied. "I've been at Mom's."

"How is Joyce?" Louise wanted to know. She had not seen Charlotte's mother in a long time.

"Same, good," Charlotte answered. "She's coming to the ceremony tomorrow," she added.

"How wonderful! I look forward to seeing her again," Louise said.

"It's not so much that you look different as it is that you look funny." Beatrice eyed her friend. "What is wrong with you?"

Jessie punched Bea in the side with her elbow. "Bea, that's no way to talk to Louise. Her husband just died."

"Oh, right," Bea responded. She kept looking at Louise. "Is that it then?" she asked.

"Is what it?" Louise asked, trying to figure out what Bea was driving at.

"No, that's not it," Bea answered herself. "Something is up with you," she said, studying her. "And it isn't grief or blushing bride stuff."

Jessie waved the comment away. "Louise, did you get everything taken care of?" she asked. She knew that their friend had remained in Maryland until all the paperwork had been taken care of. She also knew that George's daughters had been staying with her since their father's death.

Louise nodded. "It was all very dignified at the end and everything went smoothly. George and the girls reconciled before he passed and they got everything straightened out. It was all very nice," she said.

Jessie smiled. "I'm glad you could be a part of that," she noted.

"You get the house cleaned and emptied out?" Bea asked.

"Went on the market last weekend," Lou responded, still feeling Bea studying her every move. "Would you quit looking at me like that?" she demanded.

Beatrice eyed her again and then looked away.

"How do you feel?" Charlotte wanted to know.

Louise shrugged. "I don't know. It's all still so weird. Me marrying George. Me taking care of Roxie's husband, being around all of her things. Then me burying him. Being with the girls as we took care of all of the arrangements." She shook her head.

"She'd have thought it was funny," Louise added, motioning toward the gravestone. She was talking about Margaret.

Jessie smiled. "She would have laughed her butt off about all of this." She glanced down at the grave. "That's why we came, we wanted her to hear everything."

"Looks like you're having a picnic," Louise commented.

"Just a little liquid refreshment, enjoying a toast, you know," Charlotte noted with a smile. "Will you join us?"

"Of course," Louise answered.

Charlotte bent down and got another plastic cup from the stack they had just bought from the store. Then she poured some champagne from the bottle. "Cheers," Charlotte said.

Louise took a sip and smiled. "Cheers to us all," she responded.

The women picked up their plastic cups as well and took a sip.

Louise drew in a breath and glanced around and then back at Margaret's grave. "She would have loved that you and James are having a renewal ceremony, Jess. She would have wanted to walk you down the aisle." Louise moved closer to Jessie. "She may have even bought herself a new dress!"

"Well, let's not get carried away," Jessie responded. "Margaret hardly ever bought herself anything," she added.

"Yeah, but Louise is right," Charlotte said. "She would have splurged for this occasion. She would have loved this." She cleared her throat and knelt down to touch the top of the headstone.

The women were silent for a few minutes.

"I miss her so much," Charlotte said, choking back tears. "Sometimes I just wish I could hear her voice, you know?"

Jessie dropped her hand on Charlotte's shoulder. "We all miss her."

"I came out here the night before I left with George," Louise confessed. "I brought my lounge chair and just sat here talking to her for the longest time. The preacher even came out to check on me."

The women looked at Louise and laughed, recalling how she had done the same thing when Roxie died.

"You weren't drunk, were you?" Charlotte asked, remembering how Louise had taken a thermos of whiskey to Roxie's grave.

"No, not this time," she replied. "Although I did bring a martini and pour it over her on her birthday," she added with a smile. "Margaret told me she liked vodka martinis when she was young."

"She told me it was margaritas," Jessie said. "So that's what I brought her."

Charlotte laughed. "What about you, Bea? Did you douse the grave with some hooch too?"

Beatrice was still studying Louise. She wasn't paying attention to the conversation.

"Bea." Jessie nudged her.

"What?" she asked, suddenly noticing how everyone was staring at her. "What?" she asked again.

"Nothing," Charlotte replied.

The women were silent again. A few cars passed on the road beside the cemetery, and they would look up to see if they recognized anyone.

"You had sex with him, didn't you?" Bea asked.

"What?" Louise shouted back.

"George," she replied. "Did you have sex with him?"

"Beatrice," Jessie yelled. "That is none of your business!"

Charlotte started to laugh. She sat down on the grave and leaned her back against the headstone. "This I got to hear," she said, looking toward Louise. She took her cup and drank a sip of champagne.

Louise glanced at Charlotte and then back to Beatrice. "Bea, I did not have sex with George. He was terminally ill," she noted. "And I'm gay," she added. "What is wrong with you?" she asked, kicking some dirt toward her friend.

Beatrice kept watching her. "Something is different, funny," she said again. "So, if it wasn't sex, what is it?" she asked.

"Beatrice, will you leave Louise alone?" Jessie said. "She's just buried her best friend's husband and handled his estate. She's just driven from Maryland, for heaven's sake. She's tired."

"She's more than tired," Bea noted.

"I thought you gave up those cable stations," Lou said to Bea. "Didn't your mailman turn you in?"

"Eldon did not turn me in. He just delivered the bill," she said defensively.

"And how much was that bill?" Jessie wanted to know.

Beatrice took her eyes away from Louise and turned to Jessie. "It was a lot," she answered. "I'm paying it in installments," she added. "And Dick doesn't know."

Louise laughed. "And you think I'm the one hiding something?" she needled her friend. "You think I have a secret?"

"Yes, I do," Bea replied, turning back to Louise.

"Man, do I miss all of this," Charlotte said with a big grin. "I love those women at St. Mary's, but none of them are as funny as you two." She pulled her legs up and crossed them at the knees.

Jessie and Louise glanced at each other and then sat down beside Charlotte. Beatrice remained standing over them.

"You remember what Margaret used to say about having secrets?" Jessie asked, leaning against the grave marker.

"Secrets are like babies and spring flowers. It may take a long time, but sooner or later, they pop out." Louise and Charlotte recited the saying together. They looked at each other and laughed.

Louise looked up at her friend. "Beatrice, sit down here with us."

Beatrice sighed. "I can't. I have on a new pair of panty hose," she said.

"And you're worried you'll get them dirty?" Charlotte asked. "That's why we have the blanket."

"No, I'm worried that I will split them," Beatrice replied. "I had to buy a size too small because that was all they had at the boutique."

"Get your butt down here with the rest of us." Louise tugged on the hem of Beatrice's dress.

Beatrice carefully lowered herself to sit on the ground with her friends. "I don't understand why we can't sit on chairs like normal people," she complained.

"Because, Beatrice, you can call this group a lot of things, but normal is not one of them." Louise laughed and slapped her friend on the back.

"Now, Pastor Charlotte." Louise turned to the

young woman. "What is going on with you and the new man we keep hearing about?"

Beatrice snapped her head toward Charlotte to hear the answer. Charlotte immediately noticed the reaction and waited before responding. She watched Beatrice suspiciously and then turned back to Louise. "There's nothing to tell," she replied. "We broke up," she added.

"Ah, honey," Jessie said, taking Charlotte by the hand. "I hadn't heard."

"I'm sorry, Charlotte," Louise said, reaching over and patting her on the leg.

"It's okay," Charlotte said. "I just don't think a long-term relationship is in my cards."

"Why would you think that?" Jessie asked, surprised to hear her friend's comment.

Charlotte shrugged. "I just think I do better on my own, you know? It's complicated trying to work at the women's shelter and have a relationship." She pulled a blade of grass from the ground next to her.

"When did you break up?" Beatrice asked, even though she already knew the answer.

"Three weeks ago," Charlotte replied. "I broke it off."

Beatrice seemed surprised that she had answered honestly and didn't make a remark.

"And you really think it's over?" Jessie asked, sounding very concerned.

Charlotte turned to Jessie and then nodded. A

few tears stood in the corners of her eyes. She shrugged. "I'm never getting married," she said.

"Oh, honey, let me be the first to say, you can never say never." Louise reached up and hugged Charlotte.

"It'll work out," Jessie said, cupping Charlotte's chin in her hand. "You'll see," she added. "Just because this wasn't the one doesn't mean you won't find Mr. Right."

"Or as in Lou's case, Mr. Right Now," Bea said.

Louise punched Bea in the leg, causing her to tip over.

Charlotte shook her head. "I don't know. I think maybe he was Mr. Right. It's just I'm Ms. Wrong." She looked away.

No one made a comment. Charlotte cried a bit more and then wiped her eyes and nose. "Okay, this is not supposed to be a pity party," she announced. "Margaret would tell us to drink up this champagne and then leave this cemetery and go eat some cake!"

The women drank the last from their cups. Jessie nodded, and she and Louise pulled each other up. Charlotte stood up and offered Bea her hands. Bea took them and was pulling herself off the ground. As she was being helped up she turned to Louise one last time, and Louise noticed the glance.

"All right, Mrs. Beatrice Newgarden Witherspoon, now is as good a time as any to give you my news. You are right. Something has happened. Something is different!"

The three women turned to Louise, waiting.

"I'm loaded!" she exclaimed. "George left me five million dollars!"

Charlotte suddenly dropped Beatrice's hands and then looked on helplessly as Bea dropped back flat on her butt, the panty hose ripping loudly as she fell.

Navajo Fry Bread

10 cups self-rising flour
2 small packages dry yeast
warm milk (enough to mix well)

Mix ingredients well and knead into a roll of dough. Flatten dough out by hand to about ¼-inch thick. Cut into desired size and fry in hot oil until golden brown. Drain and serve with honey or jelly.

—Donovan Sanchez

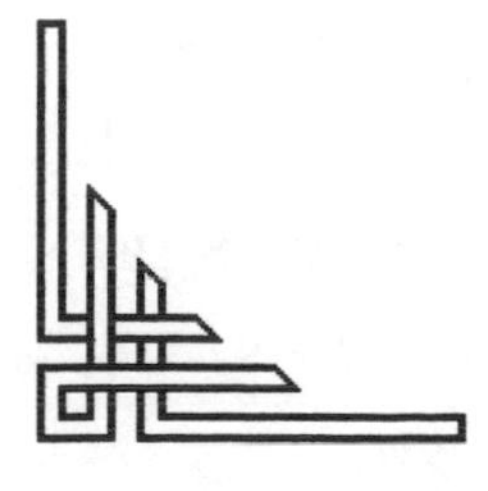

Chapter Twenty-three

"I thought Louise said he didn't have any money." James was in the front bedroom with Charlotte. She was helping him fix his tie. They were supposed to walk out of the house and into the backyard for the ceremony first. Jessie, Louise, and Beatrice, along with all the daughters and granddaughters, were in the master bedroom, putting the finishing touches on the bride, who would come out last.

The backyard at Jessie and James's house was arranged with folding chairs and one large tent with tables where the food would be served. There were tiny white lights strung in the row of apple trees that bordered both sides of the property. There was a small canopy draped in fragrant bright pink flowers at one end, which was where the wedding party would stand for the ceremony. The event had been rescheduled for a couple of months after the original date, but all the details went as planned. Beatrice had made certain that everything was handled and she had worked all morning making sure the chairs were set and the venue was perfectly arranged. The people began to gather at three-thirty in the afternoon, and the service was to begin at four. The weather was perfect, with a slight breeze for the early summer day.

“Well, that’s what she thought,” Charlotte responded. “But it turns out George was quite the investor. He bought tech stocks in the early nineties, sold them before the market dropped, bought land, sold it before the real estate crash, and anyway”—she shook her head—“I can’t remember all of the details, but I do know that she says he was worth millions.” She looked at her work on James’s tie. “Perfect,” she said with a smile.

James glanced at himself in the mirror. “You make a fine half Windsor, Pastor,” he commented.

“So he ended up changing his mind and leaving his children some money in a trust with certain restrictions or something I didn’t quite understand, and gave Louise five million, all liquidated and transferred into her bank account. Plus she gets the proceeds from the sale of the house when that goes through.” Charlotte looked in the mirror. She brushed lint from her clergy robe and straightened her wedding stole.

“Well, I just can’t believe it. Louise is loaded.” James grinned. “I can’t think of a better person to have a lot of money!”

“Yeah, it’s funny, isn’t it? The whole time she was considering taking George up on his marriage proposal she never asked about his net worth. She really never even thought about that. In fact, she had sold some of her stocks because she figured she would end up having to spend her own money on things for George." Charlotte touched at the sides of her hair. "Am I getting gray?" she asked, leaning into the mirror.

James smiled and peered down at Charlotte's head. "I think it's just the light," he said. "Has she thought about what she wants to do with the money?" he asked.

"Spread the wealth, so she says," Charlotte replied. "She's paying Bea's cable bill." She laughed.

"Well, that sounds like that might round out at a few hundred thousand," James noted with a grin. Like all the cookbook committee members, he knew about Beatrice's cable arrangement too.

"And she's going to give us a million dollars to build a new women's shelter in Gallup. I can't tell you how happy I am about that," she added.

"Jessie told me that Louise decided that last night after hearing you tell the stories about the unsafe conditions and lack of room at St. Mary's."

"She did. I was going on and on about security and how many women needed a safe place and how we had to turn some people away, and she just volunteered a million dollars." Charlotte shook her head. "I never expected it. And now I can go back to New Mexico and start working on finding land and building a new facility."

"Well, that sounds just like our Louise. She'll

more than likely give it all away and not buy herself a single thing," James responded.

"You're probably right," Charlotte agreed.

James nodded. "She's a good person, that Louise."

"One of the best," Charlotte noted. "And then there's Jessie, who was your wife and who is now to be again," she added.

James smiled and put on his suit jacket. "And to think I almost lost her," he said as he buttoned the jacket.

"You couldn't lose Jessie," Charlotte said.

"No, you don't know, Pastor," James explained. "She was very hurt when she found that letter, and I wasn't sure she'd take me back." He pulled at the sleeves of his jacket. "I should have told her about Ramona when I came home. I just didn't want to mess things up, and then so much time passed, it seemed insignificant." He placed a pocket square in his front jacket pocket. "Of course, it wasn't insignificant. And I should have told her." He shook his head. "After all we went through these past few months, I honestly didn't think this day would happen," he added.

Charlotte picked up the groom's boutonniere from the dresser, and James turned to face her while she tried to find the exact place to pin it on his jacket. "Well, this day is happening," she said, finally securing the flower and then checking to make sure it would stay. "And you are the most handsome groom I have ever seen," she commented.

"You will say that to some other man one day soon," he said. "You will have your own wedding and your own handsome groom," he added with a wink.

"I wouldn't wager on that," she responded, sounding a bit glum. "Besides, there are lots of things worse than being single."

"It's true," James noted. "But there aren't a whole lot of things better than having a partner you really love." He backed away from Charlotte and smoothed down the sides of his jacket. "I know because I've had both of those experiences, and I wouldn't choose that being single thing ever again." He shook his head as he studied his reflection.

There was a pause and James turned quickly to Charlotte, concerned that he might have hurt her feelings.

"Not that I know what's best for everyone," he said, trying to take back what had just been spoken. "Single is better than being in a horrible marriage or being like your women at the shelter and in a violent relationship. There's a whole lot worse than being alone," he added. "And I'm sure you've seen it."

Charlotte nodded. "I have," she said. "And I think that part of my problem is that those marriages are the only ones I've seen for about five years. I've only seen relationships that are poisonous at best and deadly at worst. I had forgotten until now that people can be married and love each other and be right for each other and that a marriage can be filled with the good things"—she smiled at James—"the best things in life."

James took Charlotte by the arms. "Pastor, I have seen and known a lot in my long life. I have been both pleasantly surprised and bitterly disappointed by people. I have been known to think my own thoughts of violence and destruction, and knowing that about me causes me great shame because I know I am as capable of wrongdoing and hurt as any other man I've seen or heard about. But I also know that love can quell the storms in lowly spirits and in tortured minds. Love can open closed hearts, even heal broken places. I know that for my own life, my own shut-down self, my own tumultuous soul, my own raggedy faith." He paused. "Jessie's love saved me. It saved me when I was a young man and even when I turned my back on it when I was middle-aged, it was still saving me then. And thank the Lord, I see it now and I welcome it, I want it. It is saving me again."

Charlotte could feel the tears standing in her eyes.

"And it will happen for you," James added. "I know it. It just will because you are too lovely of a woman, too beautiful of a soul, not to have it." He nodded. "You just wait. You just don't be afraid of it. Love will come back to you. It will."

The two of them embraced for a long, tender hug until finally there was a knock at the door. Charlotte pulled away and immediately reached for a tissue and began wiping her eyes. James opened the door, and Beatrice was standing there.

"Is it time, Bea?" he asked, and then glanced at his watch.

"Yes," she replied. She bit her bottom lip.

Charlotte picked up her notes and Bible and turned to face Beatrice. "What, Bea?" she asked, noticing that her friend seemed a bit uncomfortable. "Is something wrong with the sound system?" she asked.

Bea shook her head and was still biting her lip.

"Is it the photographer? Is it the musician? Jessie? What is it?"

She shook her head again. "I, uh, I made a call—" She stopped.

"Bea?" a voice called from the back room. "The flower girl needs to know her cue." It was Lana, James and Jessie's granddaughter-in-law, speaking. Hope was her daughter, and she was to come out before Jessie and scatter rose petals.

Bea faced the direction of the voice. "I'll be right there." She turned back to Charlotte. Her face was pinched and red. "I may have . . ."

"Bea, is there supposed to be a guest registry?" another voice called from the kitchen.

Beatrice shook her head and smiled at Charlotte. She cleared her throat. "You look really beautiful and we're all so glad you're here to officiate at this event. And, Charlotte, you know that I wouldn't do anything except what I do out of love, you know that, right?" she asked.

Charlotte appeared confused. "What did you do?"

"Bea!" the voice from the kitchen called out again.

"Yes, I'll be right there," she yelled. "The guest book is by the back door," she added. She waved her hand in front of her face. "I need to go," she said to Charlotte.

"Bea, wait, what is it you wanted to say?" Charlotte called out, but Bea was already heading down the hall to the back of the house.

Charlotte turned to James and both of them shrugged.

"Beatrice is a conundrum," James said, shaking his head. "But she puts on a fine wedding," he added.

"All true," Charlotte commented. "Well," she said, looking at her watch. "I guess it's time for us to go."

James moved past Charlotte through the bedroom door and she followed. They headed out of the house and at the right moment, with the appropriate song playing on the electric piano, she walked down the makeshift aisle first and James walked behind her. They both turned and faced the audience, waiting for the attendants and the bride to join them. Charlotte smiled at all the familiar faces in the audience, faces of former parishioners that she hadn't seen in a number of years. She was enjoying seeing everyone again.

It wasn't, however, until Charlotte turned her gaze and looked near the back of the house that she saw the reason Beatrice had acted so strange earlier.

He was standing near the steps. Donovan had come to Hope Springs.

Perfect Coconut Wedding Cake

3 packages frozen coconut, thawed
1 16-ounce container sour cream
2 cups sugar
yellow cake mix

Mix coconut, sour cream, and sugar in large bowl. Cover with foil and refrigerate overnight. Do not stir after mixing.

Make 2 9-inch layer cakes from yellow cake mix, using box directions. Cool and cut into 2 layers each. Spoon coconut mixture between each layer and frost top of cake. Wrap with plastic wrap and refrigerate a couple of days before cutting.

—Beatrice Witherspoon

Chapter Twenty-four

"Do you think we should be worried?" Louise whispered to Jessie as they stood under the tent enjoying the appetizers and champagne that Beatrice had catered. Everything was perfect at the reception, including the display of the small cookbooks she had placed at every table. Louise was referring to the absence of both Charlotte and Beatrice, who had disappeared after the ceremony and were apparently in the house. They were not, however, together. Lana had revealed this to Louise and Jessie after she had taken her daughter inside to change shoes. She had informed the women that Charlotte was talking to a strange man in the living room and Beatrice was on the phone with her daughter Robin, who had called her stepfather, Dick, during the service to ask that her mother call her right away.

"You're going to get a cramp if you keep straining your neck that way," James said to Jessie when he walked over to stand with his wife and her friend.

"It's Bea and Charlotte," Jessie explained. "I'm just worried that something is happening."

"Something is happening," James responded, leaning over and kissing his wife on the cheek. "Charlotte is falling in love all over again, Beatrice is taking a phone call, and we are enjoying our guests and this beautiful celebration."

Jessie smiled at her husband. She reached up and touched his cheek, kissing him.

"Would my beautiful, newly recommitted wife like to dance with me?" James asked.

Jessie glanced over at Louise.

"I'll keep my eye out," Louise responded, noticing the glance. "I'll let you know if I find out anything." She smiled at her friends. "Go dance! It's your wedding day."

Jessie and James headed off to the middle of the tent area where a small dance floor had been placed. As they walked toward the floor, the DJ announced, "Ladies and gentlemen, Mr. and Mrs. James and Jessie Jenkins." There was thunderous applause.

Louise watched the couple dance and then looked back at the house. Beatrice and Dick emerged through the back door, and Louise waited until they came toward the tent to move over to them.

"What's wrong with Robin?" she asked. She had heard about the emergency call when Dick told Bea about her call.

Bea waved away the question. "She's called off the wedding," she answered. "Farrell Monk ended up showing his true colors when they discussed having children."

Louise waited for more of the story.

"Dick, honey, would you get me a glass of sparkly?" Beatrice smiled at her husband.

He nodded and walked over to the bar.

"He told her he didn't want to have any more children and that he had in fact already had a vasectomy." Beatrice shook her head. "I knew something wasn't right about this guy."

"And all this time he hadn't ever told Robin?" Louise asked, sounding surprised.

Bea shook her head. "No. And in all this time he failed to mention that his last marriage was actually his second and not his first time at the altar."

"Poor Robin," Louise said sadly. "She must be devastated."

"Yes, she's pretty heartbroken. But she says that she's glad at least that she learned this now instead of after marrying him. She's planning to go and stay a few weeks with her sister."

Dick walked up and handed Beatrice a glass of champagne. "I see Roger Gray from the Kiwanis Club over there. I think I'll go say hello." He kissed his wife on the cheek. "You put on a beautiful wedding, hon."

She smiled at her husband. "It did turn out well, didn't it?"

"Splendid," Dick replied. "And already people are talking about the cookbooks. It was a wonderful touch." He glanced back over at his friend. "You going to be okay?" he asked.

"Yes, yes," Beatrice said. "Go mingle," she

added. "This is a party, not a funeral." She grinned. "Lord knows, you could use a change."

He pinched her on the behind and walked away. The two women watched as he moved in the direction of a table in a far corner. They saw him sit down and begin a conversation with the couple there.

"What's Robin going to do about the wedding?" Louise asked, taking them back to the previous conversation. She knew that Beatrice had been planning to leave the next day to head to her daughter's nuptials in Mexico, scheduled for the following weekend.

"Well, that's the hard part. She's past the cancellation deadline for the hotel rooms and the reception area so she loses all the deposit money and has to pay a ridiculous fee for the band and the wedding planner." Beatrice shook her head. "She's called all of her guests but she hasn't even called the hotel yet. She dreads having to hear what they're going to tell her." She took a sip of champagne. "I knew this whole destination wedding thing was a bad idea." She turned to Louise. "You want to go to Mexico?" she asked, sounding facetious.

Louise shrugged. "Maybe," she answered. "I can afford it, you know."

The two women laughed and tapped their glasses together and enjoyed sips from their champagne. They both watched as Jessie and

James danced, and Louise and Beatrice were both smiling, apparently enjoying the reception, when Louise saw Charlotte and Donovan coming out of the house and walking down the back steps. She elbowed Beatrice in the side. "You better get ready," she said, knowing that Beatrice had called Donovan without Charlotte's knowledge. Neither of them was sure how Charlotte was dealing with her ex-boyfriend's appearance in her hometown.

Beatrice cleared her throat. She steadied herself, not knowing how Charlotte was going to react.

The young couple walked up. Charlotte was smiling, and Beatrice sighed, taking the smile as a positive sign.

"Louise Fisher, this is Donovan Sanchez, from New Mexico," Charlotte introduced them.

"Nice to meet you, Donovan." Louise stuck out her hand, and he shook it.

"Nice to finally meet you too, Ms. Fisher."

"It's Louise," she said with a smile.

He nodded. "Louise," he responded.

"And you, Bea, I think have already met Donovan," Charlotte said, her voice sounding a bit stern.

"Well, yes, and it's so lovely to make your acquaintance in person, Donovan," Beatrice said with a smile.

"Donovan was telling me about your frantic phone call yesterday afternoon. Something about me being distraught and planning to go to a cemetery to drink." Charlotte looked at Beatrice. "You want to tell me about that?" she asked.

Beatrice shrugged and grinned. "I just, well, I just remember you asking us about going to see Margaret again and I was, well, I was worried that maybe you were having a breakdown of some kind."

"Right," Charlotte said.

"In her defense," Donovan said, taking Charlotte by the hand, "she was very worried about you." He smiled at Beatrice and then turned to Charlotte. "And I'm very glad she did call," he added.

Charlotte blushed and rolled her eyes at Beatrice.

The music ended, and everyone applauded as Jessie and James left the dance floor and walked over to where Charlotte and Donovan and their friends were standing. Charlotte introduced the couple to Donovan, and they greeted him with hugs and a slap on the back from James.

"It's fine to meet you, Donovan," James said to the young man he had only recently heard about.

"It's wonderful meeting all of you too," Donovan replied. "The two of you seem very happy together," he added, speaking to Jessie and James.

"We are that," Jessie noted. "Beatrice, you

outdid yourself today," she added. "The food is terrific. The music is perfect. What a wonderful, wonderful thing you did here."

"It was certainly all my pleasure," Beatrice said, enjoying the praise.

"It was a lovely ceremony," Donovan said to Jessie.

"It was, and that is, as I said, because of Beatrice's planning, and of course Charlotte's officiating," she noted. "We're so glad you came to do this, Charlotte," Jessie said with a smile. "Thank you so much."

"You're welcome," Charlotte responded. "I can't think of anything I have ever had more fun doing." She reached over and hugged Jessie.

"Well, I hope our wedding is just as lovely," Donovan said with a smile, taking Charlotte by the hand.

The group turned their gaze from Donovan to Charlotte, who leaned back from her hug with Jessie and was grinning from ear to ear. She held out her left hand to display a newly placed turquoise and diamond ring.

"He asked and I said yes!" she exclaimed.

"Well, I'll be!" Louise pulled Charlotte into a huge hug while the others clapped and shouted.

Beatrice was so stunned she couldn't say a word, and finally Charlotte wrapped her arms around her and whispered a thank-you into her ear. "For once in my life, I am very glad you meddled!" she said, and kissed her friend on the cheek.

"Have you set a date?" Jessie wanted to know.

"Will you get married here or back in New Mexico?" Louise asked.

"We both want to have a ceremony in Gallup," Charlotte replied. "Donovan is Navajo and he has an uncle who is a shaman and we'd both really like him to do the blessing. And I'd like it if the women at St. Mary's could join us." She glanced around, noticing how the group seemed a bit disappointed in the news that the wedding wouldn't occur in Hope Springs. "But we decided that we'd like to do something with all of you too. So, since we're both here, we thought we'd have our honeymoon with my friends now and then go back and have a ceremony and party in Gallup later in the year."

Jessie smiled and touched Charlotte on the arm. "I think that's a beautiful idea," she said. "It will give us some time to get to know Donovan, and maybe we can have another party here. Beatrice is pretty good at this kind of thing, you know."

"Jessie, I was worried that you and James would be heading out of town for a trip yourself. Are you planning a honeymoon of some kind?" Charlotte asked.

"We decided that we would rather spend our money on a nice vacation later in the year. We'd like to take the whole family on a trip but just not right now. And maybe since there's going to be a wedding, that will be a trip out west!" Jessie said with a smile. "Anyway, we will be right here for the next few days while the two of you have your pre-honeymoon honeymoon."

The two women hugged.

"Wait a minute!" Louise called out. "How about we all take a trip now?" she asked.

"What do you mean?" Bea was the one to ask.

"Well, what if I pay Robin back for all of her expenses incurred at her wedding resort, and the group of us, whoever would like to come along, go and enjoy what she planned?"

Charlotte appeared confused. "What are you talking about?" she asked.

"Robin is planning to cancel her wedding but she has to pay for everything because it was supposed to be next weekend."

Bea turned to Louise. "You'd really do that?" she asked. "You'd give Robin the refund?"

"Yes, and I will pay for us all to enjoy a weekend in Mexico. We'll have the engagement party, if Charlotte and Donovan want, and we'll have a honeymoon with both the soon-to-be newlywed and renewed couples." Louise grinned.

"Well, sounds like we need a toast for that," James said.

Dick came over, and after hearing the call for a toast, retrieved champagne for the young couple and for himself. When they were all ready, they raised their glasses.

"James, if I may," Louise spoke up. "Let us toast friendship and the surprise of good fortune."

"And let us honor long love, tested and true," Jessie added, smiling at her husband.

"And new love," James noted. "The opening of a heart."

"To James and Jessie and Charlotte and Donovan," Louise added.

"To us all," Beatrice said with a smile.

And everyone took a sip of champagne.

"It's time for the newly remarried couple to cut the cake," the DJ announced, and Jessie and James walked over to the table with the lovely wedding cake Beatrice had catered. They cut a slice for themselves, fed each other as pictures were snapped, and then everyone was served.

Donovan took a bite of his slice of cake and turned to the group of friends still standing near him. "This is wonderful cake," he commented. "Does anyone know the recipe?" he asked.

There was a moment of silence and then they all laughed as Beatrice gave a very satisfied grin. "I'll go and make that call to Robin," she said. "And get that lovely man a cookbook!"

Reading Group Guide

1. Were you surprised by the marriages and proposals in this book? Which one surprised you the most, and why?

2. What was your reaction to George's proposal to Louise, and to her answer? What are some of the reasons, besides love, that people marry?

3. Do you think Jessie overreacted when she discovered James had been involved with another woman while they were separated? How would you define betrayal in a marriage? Does it involve just a sexual relationship?

4. Bea's daughter leaves her mother out of the engagement and wedding plans. What do you think was the main reason for this? Do you like her idea of a "destination wedding"?

5. Are Charlotte and Donovan a good match for each other? Do you think Donovan should still feel any responsibility for his ex-wife? Why or why not?

6. Does the title of the book make you think of all the wedding cakes you've eaten? What was the best-tasting cake you've ever had at a wedding? Which was the most beautiful?

7. If you're married, talk a bit about your wedding. What do you remember most about the event? If you're not married, what are your ideas about your wedding if you intend to have one?

8. If you're married, do you remember your vows? Did you write them, or were they traditional from your religion or culture?

9. Have you ever helped plan a wedding? What was that experience like?

10. What's the most unusual wedding you've ever attended?

An Interview with Lynne Hinton

How many weddings have you officiated since becoming an ordained minister? And which ones have been your favorites?

I couldn't count the weddings I've done as a pastor and as a chaplain. But I suppose in my twenty years of being ordained I've probably been a part of seventy or eighty. Most of them have occurred in the churches where I served as the pastor, but I have to say that I prefer the outdoor weddings. Everyone always just seems more relaxed when we're outside. The weddings are usually less formal and more fun!

What kind of advice do you give the husband- and wife-to-be?

It's usually personalized to the couple and their needs or concerns but there are always common bits of advice that I share: Communicate often and well. Let the other person know when you are worried or unhappy about something. Don't let things fester! Be willing to forgive each other, and don't hold on to each other's mistakes. I also like to encourage couples to remember how they feel on their wedding day and to hold on to that magic, to remember how they feel right then so when the years pass, they can recall why they made the commitment that they made. Finally, I stress having fun with each other and making sure that "play" is a part of the marriage.

Any good cakes?

Ah, the cakes! I usually prefer the simple ones since I'm not a fan of rich frosting. The last wedding I attended, the bride made angel food cakes with a raspberry sauce. It was perfect!

Any funny wedding stories?

At a family member's wedding the best man pinned about fifty fake gold rings on the inside of his jacket. When the minister asked for the ring, he opened his jacket and asked, "Which one you like?" The look on the minister's face was priceless!

At one wedding at which I officiated, the groom, best man, and I were waiting behind the church and were supposed to enter through a side door. When I knew it was time to come in, I reached for the doorknob and discovered it was locked. I had to run around the church and get someone to walk to the front and unlock it. And then I had to run back. Let's just say that it was the fastest I've ever moved in a robe and heels!

What would be your advice to a couple planning a wedding?

Keep it simple. Make it fun. Weddings shouldn't be stressful and folks shouldn't be uptight. Make it a great party because, remember, it is a celebration!

My Most Meaningful Wedding Experience

By Lynne Hinton

Ronny and Peggy were in their early twenties when I met them. They dropped by the church where I served to ask about having their wedding there. I explained to them that we had certain requirements for nonmembers, which included having the couple attend the church a couple of Sundays, and they would need to meet with me for a few sessions. They agreed to the requirements. After attending worship at Mount Hope UCC, in Whitsett, North Carolina, they discovered that they liked the community and soon became active members. It wasn't long after I first met the two that Ronny was diagnosed with melanoma that had spread to his liver and lungs. He began aggressive treatments and the wedding was postponed. Soon it became clear that his prognosis was not good, and there were many conversations about whether marriage was the best option for them. After Ronny became terminal, the cancer having spread to his brain, they both came to me with the desire to have a wedding.

We decided to have the ceremony during a regular Sunday worship service. It was easier on them, and it seemed important to me that this young couple know that we, as their new church home, were their family and that we supported them and would care for them as they married and as they faced whatever the future held.

The entire service was about love and the commitment required in marriage and from community. The choir sang love songs, and the congregation sang hymns celebrating the family of God. The children's sermon was about marriage and my sermon was based on a Psalm that begins, "Though I walk in the midst of trouble," and goes on to say, "I will trust in God's steadfast love." And I spoke about choosing to walk together even if the path is laden with trouble and difficulty. I charged the congregation to walk with them and said that we would go this way together and in love. I spoke openly about Ronny's condition and about the love the two of them shared, as well as the love we had for them. There were tears of joy and sorrow, and I will never forget the intimate and deep connection I felt with the couple, with the gathered community. I felt like the church was really being church. Later, we enjoyed a lovely time of fellowship and, of course, cake.

It wasn't too many months later that Ronny died, his wife at his side. It is my only experience of baptizing, marrying, and burying a person. And this all occurred in the span of one year.

Almost every wedding I officiate, I think of that Sunday morning wedding and the love I witnessed between these two young people and the love we shared in the gathered community. We stood together and made a commitment to care for one another and to walk forward no matter what we knew and didn't know that was ahead. It was my most meaningful wedding and one of my most meaningful worship experiences.

LYNNE HINTON is an international interim minister in the United Church of Christ. The author of numerous novels, including *Friendship Cake*, *Hope Springs*, *Forever Friends*, and *Christmas Cake*, she lives in northeastern Washington.

www.lynnehinton.com